'You're a lot m
I expected.'

Charlotte couldn't
only knew what it
problem?'

'I thought I had it taped, but it seems like the jury just absconded again before the final verdict was in. I don't like distractions.'

'It's up to you not to be distracted, then, isn't it?'

'Precisely. And that's something I can cope with. Unless—'

Hawk must like being precise, Charlotte thought vaguely. She was trying to decide what had stirred up the butterflies again. There was something different about Hawk's voice right now. Always deep, it seemed almost liquid right now. It was rippling over Charlotte and oozing into places that set nerve-endings alight. This was crazy. She was *not* attracted to Owen Hawkins. Not like that, anyway. Charlotte almost gulped.

'Unless what?'

'Unless the distraction is mutual.'

EMERGENCY RESPONSE

Doctors... Police... Fire... Ambulance...

**Police officers and paramedics,
nurses and fire officers: meet the dedicated men
and women of the emergency services.**

**Every day is packed with drama as they race to
help others. But while they're saving lives...
they're finding love!**

**Mills & Boon® Medical Romance™
is proud to present**

**EMERGENCY RESPONSE—
the exciting new mini-series from Alison Roberts**

THE RECOVERY ASSIGNMENT

BY
ALISON ROBERTS

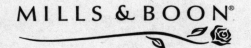

MILLS & BOON®

Special thanks to John, Nigel and especially Fiona
of the Serious Crash Unit, Christchurch branch of
the New Zealand Police force for their assistance
in the research needed for this story.

*First published in Great Britain 2004
Harlequin Mills & Boon Limited,
Eton House, 18-24 Paradise Road, Richmond, Surrey TW9 1SR*

© Alison Roberts 2004

ISBN 0 263 83933 8

*Set in Times Roman 10½ on 11½ pt.
03-1104-52890*

*Printed and bound in Spain
by Litografía Rosés, S.A., Barcelona*

CHAPTER ONE

THE picture was a long way from being pretty.

Travelling too fast to negotiate the bend in the road, the late-model, four-wheel-drive's left front wheel had left the tarmac and touched the loose shingle on the verge. A hard jerk to the right on the steering-wheel had over-corrected the error and the vehicle had begun to yaw, slipping sideways whilst still hurtling forward. The height and weight of the model had contributed to the disaster and the vehicle had tipped and then rolled. It had flipped once…twice… three times before slamming to a halt against a tree. The image was a violent one of a scarred landscape, twisted metal and potentially fatal injuries to those unfortunate enough to be inside the vehicle.

'A local resident heard the impact and went to investigate.' Senior Constable Owen Hawkins turned his gaze away from the image being projected onto the large screen. 'He then dialled triple-one and alerted the emergency services.'

Representatives of two arms of those emergency services, fire and ambulance, were listening intently to Officer Hawkins.

'The information given to the regional control centre was enough to activate the police department's Serious Crash Squad, i.e. myself and my partner, Cam.'

Ex-partner. Hawk still couldn't believe that such a tight team could have been ripped apart so easily. It hadn't been entirely *her* fault, of course, but it was easy to assign blame when one's life was getting mucked around with to this extent. Having someone other than his best mate to direct his frustration at had helped him cope over the last week or two, but right now it wasn't going to aid his current brief of improving the liaison between the SCS and other emergency services.

'What makes this a serious crash?' Owen Hawkins threw the question into the group of a dozen or so fire officers and paramedics without targeting anyone in particular.

'Vehicular rollover,' a male paramedic offered.

'Trapped occupants,' a fire officer added.

'High-speed impact.' The suggestion came from the only female present in the room, and Hawk was forced to acknowledge her in the brief silence that followed.

'How can you determine the speed?' He hadn't meant his tone to be quite so challenging. He didn't have anything against female paramedics. He didn't have anything against women in general. Hell, he *liked* women. It was just their capacity to turn lives upside down that he didn't trust. He'd got his life just the way he wanted it, thanks very much, and now—thanks to one, no, *two* women, the wheels were falling off in a big way.

'It's a rural road,' the woman responded. 'With an open-road speed limit. The vehicle was also travelling downhill into the bend.'

'Doesn't mean he hadn't slowed down.' Hawk stared back at the rather mousy-looking, bespectacled paramedic. She had a sweet smile so he didn't need to worry if he was coming across as being intimidating here: one of the men present would leap in to rescue her any second now.

To his surprise, however, the paramedic was not so easily silenced.

'The vehicle has a deformity greater than half a metre. There is compartment intrusion of more than thirty centimetres thanks to that tree crushing the driver's door. The front windscreen has a star pattern that was probably made by the driver's head. I'd be very surprised if he survived.

And if he hasn't, that makes the potential for serious injury to his passenger that much higher. Any accident involving death or major injury is serious.'

'Go, Laura!' More than one fire officer was grinning broadly.

'You'd better watch out,' someone quipped. 'She'll be doing your job for you next, mate.'

Hawk's smile failed to reach his eyes as he tilted his head to acknowledge both the impressive response to his challenge and the friendly warning. The fire officer couldn't possibly realise that he had just reinforced Hawk's simmering discontent by reminding him of what was due to happen tomorrow. He turned away, wishing he was back in his own office. Or out on the road, investigating a crash scene. Or following up a complicated line of enquiry. Anywhere he could distract himself from the unwelcome turns he was being forced to accept in his professional life. He pushed the button he held and another image appeared on the screen.

'The driver was killed instantly,' Hawk confirmed. 'And the front-seat passenger sustained severe chest and spinal injuries. There doesn't have to be a fatality before we're called in to investigate, however. As Laura said, any crash involving major injuries is serious. If the death of anyone involved occurs within twenty-eight days of the incident, then it becomes a fatal crash investigation.'

He waved at the scene now projected on the wall. The road was cordoned off by bright orange plastic cones. Police cars flanked the area that contained the wrecked vehicle, three fire appliances and two ambulances. Numerous uniformed officers could be seen at work.

'Who arrived on the scene first?' Hawk queried.

'Probably us,' a fire officer responded. 'We're quick off the mark around here.'

'Only if you're awake.' The male paramedic grinned. He

glanced at Hawk. 'It depends on current deployment of resources. Sometimes a tow truck can get to a scene before any emergency vehicles.'

'Bloody sharks,' someone muttered. 'Eavesdropping on our radio frequencies to tout for business.'

Hawk ignored the comment, though he could sympathise with the sentiment. 'In this case, the police were first to arrive with a response time of four minutes and they were able to secure the scene. The first fire truck arrived at six minutes, closely followed by an ambulance. I arrived on scene eight minutes after the call was received.'

New images appeared more rapidly. Pictures of the vehicle and the debris scattered over a long stretch of tarmac. Heavy cutting equipment being used by fire officers to extricate the victims and paramedics working to stabilise the injured passenger.

'It's imperative that both the fire and ambulance services have unrestricted access to a crash scene. The preservation of life and safety for everyone involved takes immediate priority but this does make my job more complicated because it's inevitable that a lot of evidence gets disturbed or destroyed.'

Hawk let his gaze travel right around the room. 'That's why I'm here. We're all part of an overall team and the more we understand each other's jobs, the more we can work to help rather than hinder each other.'

A senior fire officer nodded. 'We have the advantage in being a peripheral city fire station. Having fire and ambulance working from the same base has made a real difference in how we work together.'

The male paramedic mirrored the nod. 'We can tell these guys exactly what we need to get access to our patient or how we want the extrication done, and they're in there securing the vehicle or cutting the right bit from the chassis. Saving time can save lives.'

'Exactly. And if you know what we're looking for and how we work, we can save time, do our jobs better and hopefully make a contribution to general road safety. So, what is it that we do?'

The projected image was now in written form. 'There are three main threads to our investigations. The vehicle, the driver and the environment. It's helpful if we can get to a scene quickly. That way we can document road factors like traffic and weather conditions. A lot of the debris is still in place and we can talk to any witnesses or uninjured people that may have been involved. The first things said at a scene are the most likely to be factual. Victims who do not wish to appear at fault may well construct a different story later.'

'Should we be taking notes about anything said to us?'

'That's not part of your job,' Hawk told the male paramedic. 'And I wouldn't expect you to do anything that could interfere with your own protocols, but if you remember something that comes up in an interview we might have later, that's great. Same goes for impressions like the smell of alcohol or the mental state of those involved. You guys have a lot more experience than us in dealing with the kind of reactions people have to traumatic situations. If something seems odd to you, we'd like to know about it. On or off the record.'

'We get advice about what to do at a potential murder scene,' the paramedic, Laura, said. 'Like disturbing evidence as little as possible. What can we do to minimise destroying any evidence the SCS needs?'

'If you need to move something to assist a victim, do it,' Hawk responded. 'We'd just like to know about it. If you have to break windows, unlock doors or turn ignition keys off, do it but let us know.'

'What about safety belts?' a fire officer queried. 'Is it OK to cut them?'

Hawk nodded. 'In fact, it's better to cut them and leave the clip in place than to unclip it and not have that recorded. That way, we can be sure that they were wearing a seat belt.'

'Sometimes we're moving vehicle parts that we've cut. Or cargo that's come off a truck. Is that a problem?'

'The more that gets changed, the less of a full picture we're going to be able to put together,' Hawk responded. 'If we get told about the changes, we can factor them in.' He cleared his throat. 'Sometimes small things can make a huge difference. Like a pedestrian versus car scenario, for example. When a vehicle hits a person, they'll often lose a pair of glasses or a hat or handbag or something. The point at which that object falls is often the best indication of the point of impact. Some well-meaning person might pick the item up to give it back to the victim or tidy up a scene and that can make it impossible to be sure exactly where the victim was standing. And that could make the difference between the accident being the fault of the victim or the driver.'

Hawk's face was serious as he let his gaze rest on Laura. She stared back and Hawk had the uncomfortable feeling that he was being evaluated for more than the content of his talk. He could feel some of the warmth leach out of his tone. 'Fatal accidents can become court cases for manslaughter. A car is just as much of a lethal weapon as a gun in the wrong hands. Even small pieces of evidence can become of vital importance.'

His audience was clearly impressed, with the exception of Laura who was looking as though he had just scored another black mark on some personal score sheet. Hawk shrugged mentally and moved on, his tone now impersonal as he changed the image on the screen again.

'What specifically are we looking for from the environment?' He ran through a series of close-up photographs of tyre marks on road surfaces. 'These can all tell their own story,' he commented. 'A yaw mark is a skid in a large arc and you'll see these distinctive cross-marked tread patterns or striations. An acceleration scuff will have scrape marks in the opposite direction to travel whereas braking will give you scuffing in the same direction as travel.

'Gouge marks, like this...' Hawk pointed to the crescent shape carved into tarmac '...indicate the point of contact during a vehicle rollover. The mark occurs as the wheel rim hits the road. In this one—' the crescent mark had a perfect circle close by '—the circle has been made by the central hub of the wheel during the final rollover.'

The next picture looked as though someone had emptied a rubbish container along a stretch of road. Papers, beer cans, broken glass, items of clothing and children's toys were strewn over a surprisingly large area.

'Debris scatter indicates the direction of travel of a vehicle and, potentially, its speed,' Hawk told them.

He reached into a cardboard carton at his feet a few minutes later. The presentation was going smoothly and he was looking forward to finishing. He really wasn't in the mood for liaison duties and that in itself was annoying. This kind of job had been a favourite when he and Cam had made it a joint effort. They could kick back and enjoy a semi-social occasion with their colleagues from complementary emergency services. There'd be jokes and laughter and maybe a beer or two at a local pub afterwards. If Laura had been scowling suspiciously at Cam he would have charmed her into appreciation pretty fast and it would have given the partners a moment of shared amusement later.

But those days were gone. As far as Hawk was concerned he was going solo now. He might be about to have a new partner foisted on him but that didn't change anything. Cam was irreplaceable. They had worked—and played—as two halves of a whole. No one was going to step into that position easily. The notion that a *female* officer could replace what he'd had with Cam was about as likely as hell freezing over.

The item Hawk was now handing out to the group was an example of the kind of evidence they collected from the vehicles involved in a serious crash.

'Look at the speedometer,' he instructed. 'Sometimes, with a high-energy impact, the speedo will become locked at the speed at which the vehicle was travelling. This one didn't but if you look closely you might notice something.'

The dial was being carefully scrutinised by none other than Laura. 'There's a little mark,' she observed. 'At 190 kph.'

Hawk nodded. 'A needle tap,' he confirmed. 'And another accurate indication of the vehicle's speed.'

A collective whistle came from the group.

'Didn't come from your car, did it, Cliff?' a fire officer called. 'That time we were at the pub and you realised you'd forgotten your wedding anniversary and had three minutes to get home?'

'Nah.' Cliff shook his head ruefully. 'I was late, man. Took me a month to get out of the dog box.'

'And another week to get back in.' A tall, blond fireman, who looked like an ex-surfer, was grinning broadly. 'That's marriage for you.'

Hawk joined in the laughter despite, or perhaps because of, Laura's faintly disapproving expression. He agreed with the sentiment wholeheartedly, anyway. Not that he had anything against female companionship. He never left too long a gap between his relationships, but he had it all worked out now and he knew precisely when it was time to call it quits. The first hint that the relationship was interfering with his own life or work was an alarm bell he never ignored.

Why the hell hadn't Cam recognised those signals? They'd talked about it often enough. They'd watched their friends and colleagues move in and out of serious relationships. The fact that they'd both been burnt in the past had made them an ideal team to help pick up the emotional pieces when it all went to custard—as it invariably did. They had congratulated themselves on keeping their own lives in order in that department. They'd had it all. Great careers, a partnership that had only increased in strength over the years they had been together, an ability to attract female companionship whenever they'd felt the need and, more importantly, the wisdom to hear those alarm bells and act on them.

Hawk had tried to warn him that time he'd called off a night at the rifle range to take Cassie out.

'She's interfering, mate,' he'd said sadly. 'If you don't watch out you'll be up to your eyeballs in nappies and mortgages.'

And Cam had laughed. 'Just wait.' He'd grinned. 'One of these days *you'll* fall in love again and then you'll change your tune.'

'You've been ''in love'' before, too. You know as well as I do that it never lasts.'

'This is different,' Cam had insisted. 'This is the *real thing*, Hawk.'

As if. Hawk had learnt the hard way that falling in love was an illusion. Just out-of-control hormones, and Hawk never let himself lose control of anything to that extent any more. Hadn't done for years now. No. The hormones wore off and there you were, saddled with responsibilities that changed your life. They ruined spontaneity, kept you poor and made you settle for security instead of excitement.

He'd seen people cut their careers off at the knees in order to stay put and cruise. Their energy got sucked into dealing with those responsibilities and often it wasn't until they escaped that ambition resurfaced. They got distracted, slowed down and occasionally even broken. It wasn't going to happen to Owen Hawkins.

Not in a million years.

'Take a look at these bulbs.' Hawk pulled another item from the box and stepped towards the fire officers as the laughter faded. 'When a light's on and the filament is hot at point of impact, you'll get that kind of distortion. Great physical evidence.'

The tall, blond fireman was still smiling as he reached out to take the bulb. A corner of Hawk's mouth curved slightly. He could bet the fireman wasn't married. He looked far too happy. And Hawk hadn't missed the way Laura's gaze had veered at the sound of his laughter. She did have a lovely smile and she looked…homely was the best word Hawk could come up with. Comfortable, maybe. Honest, anyway. She wasn't the type to adopt a flashy image and pretend she wanted nothing more than a good time, only to start sinking emotional claws into her male companion. Manipulating unsuspecting guys into losing control and then taking over their lives and futures.

'The position of the switches must be important.'

'Sorry?' Hawk was jerked back from the now familiar, but definitely unfair, line of thought. He couldn't blame Cassie. It had been Cam's choice and he had jumped more than willingly.

'For the lights and so forth,' the fire officer expanded. 'We should keep that in mind when we're crawling around inside cars. We probably turn things off by leaning on them without even noticing.'

'You don't even have to lean to turn things off, Stick,' someone quipped. 'Isn't that right, Laura?'

Laura laughed but flushed slightly.

'Stick?' Hawk raised an eyebrow at the solid figure now handling the row of light bulbs mounted on the narrow wooden board.

'He got hit with an ugly one,' his companion explained.

'Oh.' Had Laura rejected an advance, maybe? Not that he was remotely interested but at least a relationship between people working from the same base was reasonable. Hell, even living in the same country seemed reasonable now. If Cam had to allow his brains to get addled by a woman to that extent, why did he have to choose one that lived on the other side of the world? And why didn't she move permanently to New Zealand instead of expecting Cam to follow her home to the States like some lovesick puppy?

Hawk knew why. It was all part of the manipulation that came so naturally to the female of the species. It wasn't evil. They probably didn't even know they were doing it half the time, but the effect was the same. It was a take-over bid. The undermining of a man's independence and self-esteem. They got you right where they wanted you... and then what? 'Sorry, buddy, but I've changed my mind.' Or, 'I've found someone better than you.'

Cassie had better not treat Cam that badly. Sure, she had looked as besotted as Cam but she'd been married before, and that hadn't lasted long, had it? Cam had been married before as well. They should both have known better. Still, the fact that Cam was being uprooted to such an extent might even be the saving of his mate. He'd realise what he was giving up, get over the infatuation and come back. The desertion of his career and the principles on relationships they had espoused so enthusiastically in recent years was probably only temporary.

And that gave *him* the perfect excuse not to allow any fill-in partner to interfere or gain too much of a foothold in his department. She was going to be totally unsuitable and Cam would be welcomed back in a month or two. Hawk just had to grit his teeth and put up with it. He could do that. In fact, now that he was confident it was only temporary, it didn't seem that bad any more.

Hawk finished his session by fielding questions.

'How much time do you guys have to spend in court?'

'Quite a bit,' Hawk responded. 'Some cases can drag on if someone's lost their licence or their livelihood by being blamed for an accident. Or if an insurance company won't pay up or a family is determined to clear someone's name.'

'Who does the detective work?'

'We can end up doing quite a lot of it,' Hawk said. 'We visit the scene and mark evidence and take photographs and measurements. We oversee the vehicle inspection and call in any experts we might need for an opinion on, say, tyres or mechanical faults. And we conduct interviews.'

'Who with?'

'The driver or passengers. We might liaise with the hospital initially until we can talk to them. We talk to families and friends, witnesses and often a lot of other people. A GP might be interviewed if the driver had a medical condition. A mechanic could be asked for input if the vehicle had had any recent repairs. We'll often talk to members of the fire and ambulance services, especially if we're having any problems reconstructing a scene. That's where noting things that were moved or damaged during the incident becomes important. As do your unbiased views of what you saw. We respect your roles and value your input.'

Hawk smiled. His mood was lifting steadily now and a glance at his watch told him it was time to head home. A new watch would be clocking in at Inglewood station at 6 p.m. and he could see the first arrivals manoeuvring in the car park outside. A session in the pub with some of these guys could be just what he needed. It didn't have to be a male-only session either. He didn't mind at all if Laura came along. She was clearly a popular member of this group. One of the boys, probably, and no threat to anyone, either professionally or personally. Hawk could only hope that his new temporary partner would be from the same career-oriented mould with little interest in accentuating her femininity.

With a bit of luck she might even be built like the back of a brick outhouse and have a slight problem with facial hair. Hawk picked up the board of light bulbs and fitted them inside the box with a sigh. No, that thought was even more unappealing than having to contend with a willowy Barbie clone who couldn't possibly inspire any professional respect. He just didn't want to work with a female, dammit!

He didn't want to work with another guy either. His previous partner had been a guy. Perfectly competent as far as the job went but the lack of anything in common on a personal level had kept them purely colleagues. And even that had fallen apart when he'd discovered what a jerk the guy had been in his private life. Nobody could abuse and abandon a wife and kids in favour of an affair with a bimbo half his age and remain acceptable on any level.

No. He didn't *want* a new partner—of either gender. He wanted Cam back. His mate. Someone he could bounce ideas around with and know that the input from both sides carried equal weight in terms of experience and intelligence. Someone who understood the attraction of blondes, both willowy and curvaceous, and would empathise with the kind of hassles that took periodical sorting out when the current choice needed replacing. Someone who could smash a squash ball, fire a gun or down a few pints in front of a rugby game when time out was needed.

Hawk's response to the thanks from various members of his audience was a trifle perfunctory. The Cam he knew was gone. His mates—possibly even his career—had been dumped in favour of a short, bouncy redhead who never drank beer, hated guns and couldn't understand the rules of rugby.

'The talk was great. I learned a lot.'

'You're welcome.' Hawk looked up from shutting down the projector and nodded at Laura. 'The more we know about how each other works, the more we can help each other.'

'Maybe you should come out on the road with us sometime, then.'

His glance was more deliberate this time but he relaxed when he decided this wasn't some kind of a come-on. Laura looked like a nice person but she was definitely not his type. She was several inches too short, way too…solid and her hair was dead mouse. He could work with someone like her, though. She looked intelligent. Or was that just the impression the spectacles bestowed? Hawk was annoyed at himself at even making such a judgement. He had been doing it for days now, with every stranger he met— especially women. What would *she* be like to work with? What would his new partner be like? It wasn't that he was nervous about it. It was the sheer inconvenience of having to go through that learning curve. Trying to adapt to someone else's methods and having the job done far less efficiently because mindsets were too disparate. That was what bothered him most about trying to work with a female officer. How could they possibly be on the same wavelength, the way he and Cam had been? Hawk's foul mood settled over him again like a wet blanket.

'Good idea,' he said dismissively. 'But impractical. With a two-person unit we're basically on call on a permanent basis, and I'm currently working on my own anyway.'

'You're based at the Grisham Road station, aren't you? Covering the north and east sectors?'

'That's correct.' Hawk was almost packed up now. The flow of men around them was increasing as the shift changed. He was ready to leave and no one had suggested a quick drink. Unless that was what Laura was leading up to. Hawk's gaze flicked over the paramedic almost involuntarily. No chance—especially in his current mood. Glancing back to her face, Hawk was surprised to see the hint of a smile. If the message had been received, the interpretation certainly hadn't caused her any distress.

'Maybe the pressure will come off a bit when you get a new partner.'

The upward movement of Hawk's dark eyebrows was also involuntary. 'How do you know I'm getting a new partner?'

'You said you were working on your own…currently.'

'Hmm.' Hawk picked up his box and moved towards the door, acknowledging farewells as he went. Annoyingly, Laura was following him to the car park.

'I also happen to know your new partner.'

That stopped him. Hawk dumped the box on the front passenger seat of the squad car and turned. Laura was smiling more broadly now.

'Charlotte and I did our paramedic training together. She's my best friend. In fact, she should be unpacking the rest of her gear at my house right now. She's moving in with me until she gets settled back in Wellington…and her new job.'

'She'd better not get too settled.' The remark popped out before he could help it.

'Oh?'

Hawk had the chance to retract, or at least explain, the unfriendly comment but he didn't want to. He wasn't about to lay out any welcome mat.

'My partner has only taken a three-month leave of absence. I'm expecting him back.'

'Three months is quite a while. You may find you like working with Charlie.'

'Oh?' The sound reflected Laura's previously dubious

tone. *Charlie?* Anyone called 'Charlie' probably *was* built like a brick outhouse.

'She's very good at her job. She's just been awarded a medal of commendation.'

'So I heard.' Hawk slammed the passenger door of his car.

'She was awarded "Paramedic of the Year" two years in a row.'

Hawk was pulling open the driver's door but his head turned swiftly. He didn't want to hear how great Charlotte Laing was. She was choosing this. *He* wasn't. He was going to be spending more hours than he cared to count in her company. Sharing his small office. Hell, it was *his* life that was being turned upside down and he had no choice but to accept it. He had no control and that's what he hated most. He didn't even have Cam around to try and thrash him on the squash court and get rid of his frustration that way. The only outlet available was standing in front of him.

'So why did she change careers, then?' Hawk snapped. 'Does she have trouble making up her mind?' His snort was derogatory. 'I suppose it *is* a woman's prerogative.'

Hawk could feel the assessment in the stare he was subjected to. The judgement being made was hardly likely to be complimentary but he didn't give a damn.

'Charlotte's fiancé was killed in a car accident two years ago. The Serious Crash Squad screwed up the investigation and he got blamed for the crash that also killed two other people.'

Hawk said nothing as he eased long legs under the steering-wheel. He dismissed the automatic flash of sympathy for someone who had gone through a particularly rough patch. So somebody had made a mistake. It happened.

'Charlie became involved with the investigation. She also became convinced that if the SCS did its job well enough, they had the potential to prevent other accidents happening.'

'Accidents are acts of God,' Hawk muttered. 'We investigate crashes.' 'Charlie' had better not be about to step onto his patch expecting him not to be doing his job well enough.

Laura ignored the mutter. 'She started out as a cop before she joined the ambulance service. It didn't require much retraining to get up to speed and she hasn't let her paramedic qualifications slip either. She carries a full kit and if she gets to a scene first, she can use whichever role she needs to.'

'You can't do two jobs at the same time.' The only input Hawk had managed to get into this appointment had been challenging the suitability of Cam's replacement. He'd hunted for something to argue about, dammit, and that paramedic qualification had been the best he could find. Not that it had carried the slightest weight. His complaints about both the gender and the qualifications of his temporary partner had earned him nothing more than a reprimanding glance from his boss.

'Try telling that to the last driver whose life she saved. He would have died if they'd had to stand back and wait for an ambulance.'

Hawk turned the ignition key. Laura sounded quite ready to continue defending her friend but he wasn't interested in second-hand information. He could make up his own mind.

And if the way he was feeling right now was anything to go by, he probably already had.

'Rather you than me, that's all I've got to say.'

'Oh, no, you don't.' Charlotte Laing pointed her fork at Laura. 'You can't tell me you've met the man I'm going to be working with for the next three months and then not tell me what he's like.'

'He's a cop. He seems to know what he's talking about. He's probably very good at his job.' The two women were sitting at a small kitchen table and Laura turned her attention firmly back to the plate in front of her. 'This lasagne is great, Charlie. Your cooking's improved an awful lot since we last flatted together.'

'Don't try and change the subject,' Charlotte ordered. 'I heard a rather large "but" in there somewhere. You didn't like him, did you?'

'I don't have to work with him,' Laura said calmly. Her lips quirked mischievously. 'Thank goodness.'

'Aha!' Charlotte sounded satisfied. 'So what's wrong with him?'

'He's…' Laura seemed lost for an appropriate adjective. 'He's not…very friendly.'

'Meaning?'

Laura took in her friend's intense gaze and rolled her eyes. 'OK, you asked for it. I think he's conceited and arrogant and intolerant.'

Charlotte grinned. 'Don't hold back on me, now.'

Laura chuckled. 'I just got the strong impression that he's not keen on working with a new partner and he's particularly not keen on working with *you*.'

Charlotte's jaw dropped. 'He hasn't even met me!'

'He thinks you can't make up your mind about what job you want to do. Whether you want to be a paramedic or a crash investigator. He made some derogatory remark about it being a woman's prerogative to change her mind.'

'Whoa!' Charlotte was grinning now. 'This could mean war.'

'He also expects his partner to come back. He doesn't want you getting your foot too far in the door.'

'That's not what I heard when I went in to collect my uniform today.' Charlotte scooped up the last forkful of her dinner. 'I heard that his partner, Cam, fell head over heels in love with an American woman and he's followed her home with the intention of gaining permanent residence in the States or getting married. Whichever comes first.' She reached for her glass of wine. 'I also heard that Officer Hawkins has been like a bear with a sore head ever since Cam defected.'

'That might explain the anti-woman attitude I picked up,' Laura conceded. 'It's not going to help you enjoy the job, though.'

'I can handle it,' Charlotte declared. 'Owen Hawkins can't stop me doing the work to the best of my ability, and three months should be quite long enough to prove I'm up to scratch. Then I'll be able to request a transfer to another squad.'

Laura nodded as she put her fork down and then sighed as she looked at her empty plate. 'That was delicious but that cheese sauce is going to land straight on my hips. I can feel it oozing in there as I speak.' She looked up and shook her head. 'I wish I knew how you could eat like that and stay so skinny.'

'I'm only skinny because I'm so tall. It's all stretched out.'

Laura watched Charlotte as she stood up and moved to rinse her plate at the kitchen sink. Tall and lean, Charlotte moved with a confident and fluid grace that provoked a thoughtful frown from her friend.

'You look a bit like him.'

'What? Is he effeminate or something?' Charlotte's eyes widened. 'Don't tell me he's not keen on working with a woman because he's gay.'

'No way!' Laura said dismissively. 'I just meant your build. He's tall and lean as well and you've both got black hair. His eyes are blue, though, not brown.'

'Hazel,' Charlotte corrected. 'Jamie used to tell me my

eyes reminded him of the decanter of sherry his grand-
mother always had sitting on the sideboard.'

There was a moment's silence and then Laura spoke
softly.

'You still miss Jamie, don't you?'

Charlotte sat down at the table again. 'I always will,' she
said simply. 'I doubt that I'll fall in love again. I'm
never going to meet anyone who could hold a candle to
Jamie.'

'You're only thirty-two, Charlie. You can't give up yet.'

'You haven't even hit thirty,' Charlotte countered. 'And
what was it you said about men in general when you finally
walked out on John?'

'Yeah, well. I was feeling miserable. Even though it was
a bad relationship, it was still hard getting out of it. Of
course I wasn't feeling like rushing into another one.'

'And now?'

'It's been six months. I'm over it. If I find someone who
wants me as a woman instead of a mother figure cum
housekeeper then I'm quite prepared to try again.'

'That's the difference,' Charlotte said slowly. 'What you
had wasn't good enough. You're bound to find something
better. What Jamie and I had was perfect. I couldn't replace
that no matter how hard I looked.'

'So you won't even try?'

The head shake was decisive. 'I'm not remotely interested. I'm a career-woman now. Did Officer Hawkins make
any comments about multi-tasking along with mind-
changing prerogatives?'

'He wasn't thrilled with the notion of trying to do two
jobs at once.' Laura smiled at her friend. 'But I'm sure if
he repeats any of it in front of you, he'll live to regret it.'

Sherry-coloured eyes gleamed. 'I'm looking forward to
starting this job even more now.' Charlotte flicked the end
of a long, glossy black braid over her shoulder. 'A challenge is precisely what I'm hoping for.'

CHAPTER TWO

IT WAS going to be a challenge all right.

The bid to assert control was right there in the moment of introduction. Senior Sergeant Lance Currie spotted Owen Hawkins in the corridor ahead of them as he escorted Charlotte to her office.

'Hawk—slow down for a minute. I want you to meet your new partner.'

Hawk's reluctance to be distracted from an important mission was clearly evident as the tall figure stopped abruptly, hesitated for just a fraction of a second and then turned. A disinterested expression faltered as he caught sight of Charlotte but he collected himself quickly.

Charlotte gave no hint that she had observed and inter-preted his astonishment. She was used to the effect she often had on men. The only effect it ever had on her these days was to harden her resolve to prove herself profession-ally. In this case, however, it could be to her advantage. Owen Hawkins might find her sexually attractive. She could easily score a few points in any bid for equality by letting him know she wouldn't be returning the interest.

'Hawk, I'd like to introduce you to Charlotte Laing.' Lance's raised eyebrows suggested that he might have seen that flash of involuntary reaction as well. 'Charlie, this is Owen Hawkins.'

'Charlotte.' The tone of the surprisingly deep voice was cool. There was no suggestion of a smile and the grip of his hand was a shade too firm. Charlotte squeezed right back.

'Owen.' She smiled politely. 'Pleased to meet you.' The use of his real name was deliberate. Nicknames denoted a relationship of some kind. They needed an invitation for use unless one wanted to appear patronising, and Charlotte already had the distinct impression that trying to patronise this man would get her absolutely nowhere. She held the eye contact unwaveringly, however. He looked fierce rather than mean, she decided. Focussed. Intelligent and...wary. 'Call me Charlie,' she added, injecting a little warmth into her smile as she withdrew her hand. 'Everybody does.'

She expected a reciprocal invitation to call him 'Hawk' but annoyingly it was not forthcoming. As a means of putting her in her place it was a subtle move and Hawk managed to make it seem an oversight by changing the subject.

'Sorry to be in a rush but I'm on my way to a job. I'll give you the grand tour when I get back.'

'Take Charlie with you.' Lance's suggestion was more like a command. 'She's starting work today so we may as well throw her in the deep end.'

Apparent analysis of the pros and cons took only a microsecond. 'Sure. Why not?'

And Hawk was moving again. His long legs covered the length of the corridor with a speed that would have made anyone else appear to scurry. With this man the movement gave the impression of calm assurance. Charlotte was grateful her own legs were long enough to keep up without effort. Hawk was only a couple of inches taller than her 5' 11''. She stayed just half a pace behind Hawk, however. That way she could watch him unobtrusively. She was adding tiny snippets of information with every glance. Later she would be able to collate them and decide just what she thought of her new partner.

It was no wonder Laura had been intimidated. Charlotte hadn't seen him smile yet and that didn't give any impression of warmth. He exuded assurance but it was too soon to make any judgement on whether that tipped over into arrogance. Charlotte was not going to make any error in underestimating his intelligence either. The way his face was put together—the clear, strong lines of his features and the impression that nothing escaped those dark eyes—was enough to warn her that she might well have met her match on an intellectual level.

'This way.' Hawk pushed open a smoke stop door and led Charlotte on a brisk journey down several flights of concrete stairs.

The intimidation must have been enough to blind Laura to the man's physical attributes, Charlotte decided. He looked as though he had stepped, temporarily, out of the leading role of some adventure movie. A rugged hero who could save the day and any damsels in distress along the way. The crisp, white shirt and dark trousers of his uniform hung and clung to a lean but powerful frame, and Charlotte was getting a good view as she trotted down the stairs behind him. The awareness of such masculinity was irritating. It wasn't attraction, just…awareness, but that in itself was disconcerting. Easily dismissed, though. Charlotte hadn't been remotely attracted to any man since Jamie. And she wasn't about to be now.

Hawk held the heavy door at the end of the next short corridor open and waited for Charlotte to pass him. She did so without thanking him for the courtesy. Would he have done that if he was leading the way for a male colleague?

'My squad car's here.' Hawk wrenched the door open. '*Our* car,' he corrected himself grudgingly. He glanced briefly at Charlotte—the first eye contact since their introduction. 'You do drive?' he queried.

'Of course.' Charlotte slid into the passenger seat of the station wagon and reached for her safety belt.

'Advanced driving, I meant. Have you had emergency response training?'

'Of course,' Charlotte repeated. 'I'd hardly be in a position to do this job if I hadn't, would I?'

Hawk didn't bother responding. He activated the car's beacons and had the siren going as soon as they cleared the ramp from the basement garage. More than one car on the busy road skidded slightly as the drivers braked hard. Hawk slipped the squad car into the gap and then cruised into the middle of the road, putting his foot down on the accelerator as he shot forward between the opposing lines of early morning, inner-city traffic. He knew precisely how well he could do this and he knew he was better than most. Even well-seasoned officers were known to go a little pale when they were his passengers in an emergency response and Hawk had no inclination to tone things down for Charlie.

He stole a sideways glance after negotiating a particularly narrow gap between a crowded bus and a concrete-mixing truck. The faces flashing past in the bus had shown horror at the gap of only inches between the vehicles. Charlotte, however, looked unperturbed.

'What are we going to?' she asked.

'Car versus lamppost that appears to have been fatal. There was bystander CPR on the driver getting started when the call came in.'

'Driver collapse, maybe?'

'I don't make assumptions before I arrive at a scene.'

'Do you need a map reference?' Charlotte's tone was now as clipped as his had been.

'No.'

Hawk concentrated on negotiating a rapid route through increasingly snarled-up traffic. An accident at this time of day had a surprisingly wide-reaching flow-on effect. Or maybe it wasn't so surprising. Throw a stationary fire truck or two and an ambulance into even a three-laned highway and there wasn't much space to channel traffic through. There would be police cars as well with officers trying to keep the scene clear and directing irritated motorists to a new route if possible.

Hawk was feeling a little irritated himself. The early callout had presented a welcome opportunity to delay the inevitable meeting with his new partner. He hadn't expected the mid-corridor ambush but he knew better than to refuse a direction from Lance Currie unless he had a very good reason. His boss had held the senior position at Grisham Street station for many years. He was known behind his back as Elsie, and the nickname was appropriate for more than his initials. Currie was a bit of an old woman when it came to following regulations, observing protocols and dotting every 'i' on paperwork. If he'd decided Hawk was to take his new partner out on the job then it wouldn't have been worth the repercussions if he'd refused.

Charlotte Laing had been even more unexpected than the ambush. Any hope that the potential distraction of working with a woman would be mitigated by her unattractiveness had been felled in a somewhat gut-wrenching swoop. This woman would turn heads anywhere. The only saving grace was that she was totally unlike the type of women Hawk preferred. He liked his female companions to be fun and they were invariably blonde, curvy and at least a little bit bouncy. Fluff, in other words. Charlotte Laing was as tall and slim as a pencil. Long, straight black hair twisted into a rope that only narrowed as it reached her waist. Her features were defined enough to appear almost sharp and her olive skin hinted at some exotic bloodline in her family tree. She looked, Hawk had to admit, like some native American princess and the overall effect was unusual enough to have been startling.

Hawk turned off the siren as their progress slowed to a crawl. He eased the car onto a footpath to skirt a line of cars that had no hope of manoeuvring to let them through. Pedestrians flattened themselves against a fence as a blip on the siren warned them what was happening. Hawk could see the flashing lights of other emergency vehicles in the distance but even now it was hard to concentrate solely on the task ahead of them.

It was more than irritating. Hawk had only been in her

company for about ten minutes and it was already proving difficult to fight the distraction. He'd never seen anyone like her. On the positive side, being thrown into a job with her meant that he couldn't escape. The startling effect would wear off more quickly and at least he knew there was no possibility of being distracted by a genuine attraction to the woman. No hint of bounce there. Or even a sense of femininity. Charlotte's clear, golden-brown eyes advertised steely determination and a brain that was active enough to mean he needed to stay on his toes. That game-playing scenario with their names hadn't gone over her head and Hawk had the uncomfortable feeling that he hadn't actually scored any points at all.

A police officer let Hawk's vehicle through the cordon and pointed towards a potential parking area behind a fire truck. An ambulance was parked at right angles to the fire appliance, its back doors open towards the car crumpled against the concrete post. Hawk glanced at the body lying between the ambulance officers. The man's clothing had been cut to expose his chest. A male paramedic was taping an IV line to one arm. He lifted his hands and leaned back on his heels as the other paramedic pressed paddles onto the victim's chest. Hawk grimaced at the convulsive jerk their patient made.

'Doesn't look very good,' he muttered.

'They're defibrillating him so at least there's some sign of cardiac electrical activity.'

'What?' Hawk's head swivelled. He'd forgotten he wasn't with someone who knew as little as he did about medical matters. 'I thought they only zapped people if the heart had stopped. Flat-line stuff.'

'Shocking someone can only interrupt and potentially reset the electrical activity. If there's a flat line on the screen it means there's no signal present so shocking someone isn't going to do anything other than burn a bit of heart muscle.'

'Oh.' Hawk didn't enjoy feeling ignorant. In future, he was going to keep his mouth shut and save himself a lecture.

'The heart *has* stopped in that it's not functioning as a pump, though,' Charlotte added. 'It's usually fibrillating, which is a kind of fast wiggle that can't produce an output—which is what creates a pulse.'

'So that's why it's called a *de*fibrillator.' The annoyance of having his lack of knowledge exposed was replaced by a flash of satisfaction in learning something new. Hawk shook his head. 'I'd never even thought about it.'

'Why should you have? We gain expertise in what we're trained in.'

'Exactly.' Hawk's glance at Charlotte was speculative. 'So are we going to get on with our job or do you want to go and help out with the victim?'

'That's my flatmate, Laura,' Charlotte responded. 'She and her partner, Tim, are both paramedics. They know what they're doing.'

'What *are* they doing?' Hawk stared through the windscreen as he opened his door. He hadn't recognised the paramedics who had been listening to his talk yesterday. Funny, Laura looked far less mousy performing her duties. She looked competent...and busy.

'Laura's intubating him. It secures the airway and makes breathing for the patient far more effective.' Charlotte pushed her door shut. 'Let's see if they have anything to tell us before we start on the scene, shall we?'

Hawk usually stayed well away from any paramedics when they were obviously occupied with trying to save someone's life. His protocol dictated reporting in to any senior police or fire officer on scene to start gathering information, but Charlotte had already stepped towards the paramedics and Laura had spotted her.

'Hi, Charlie! You're on the job early.'

'No time like the present. This is my partner, Owen.'

Laura tied the tape securing the endotracheal tube in place. She attached the ambubag and then glanced up briefly as she pulled her stethoscope from around her neck.

'We met yesterday.' She nodded. 'Hi, Owen.'

Hawk simply nodded. He hated being called Owen.

'Do you need a hand?' Charlotte asked.

'You could bag him while I draw up some drugs...if Owen can spare you, that is. Back-up should only be a minute or two away.'

Charlotte glanced at Hawk, clearly requesting permission to give assistance, and to his surprise, Hawk found himself nodding. It was only for a minute or two after all and he could easily use the time to gain an overall impression of the scene.

Laura was silent for a few seconds as she squeezed the ambubag and checked for air entry by listening over both sides of the man's chest with her stethoscope. 'We'll go into Emergency under CPR if necessary but I'm still hopeful. It could be that he was unconscious for a while before actually arresting. Bystander CPR was initiated quickly and he was still in coarse VF by the time we arrived.'

'VF?' Hawk couldn't help exposing his ignorance again.

'Ventricular fibrillation.' Charlotte gave him a quick glance. 'The worst kind of wiggle. The finer it is, the closer to a flat line it is. If it's coarse there's more chance of converting it to a useful rhythm.' She turned back to Laura. 'Was the arrest witnessed?'

'Kind of.' Laura's partner, Tim, had restarted chest compressions. 'The car was seen to pick up speed as it came downhill and it veered across the other two lanes and left the road. It cut one car off and the witness said that the driver appeared to be slumped over the wheel.'

'Who was the witness?'

'That guy over there in the pinstripes. He was the one who made the triple-one call. He started the CPR as well as soon as they got him out of the car. He's a bit shaken up,' Laura added. Her smile at Charlotte was sympathetic. 'You might like to tell him what a great job he did.'

'I'll go and talk to him,' Hawk said. Another ambulance was pulling up and he felt out of place. So much for his statements from only yesterday about being on the same team and the desirability of knowing as much as possible about how each branch of the emergency services did their jobs. If Hawk had been that interested in what paramedics did, he would have become one himself, instead of joining the police force. Knowing each other's jobs too well meant that it was possible to step in and assist instead of getting on with what they were supposed to be doing.

As Charlotte was demonstrating so ably. A second shock had elicited a normal but very slow heartbeat. Charlotte was handling supplies from the paramedic kit with the ease of complete familiarity. Her long fingers were snapping ampoules and drawing up drugs into syringes. Hawk found himself mesmerised for a split second. Her fingers were as long and elegant as the rest of this woman. The flash of curiosity regarding what they might feel like touching his body came from absolutely nowhere and it was as startling as it was disturbing.

It was easy to summon anger to blanket such an undesirable emotion. This was precisely what Hawk had feared might happen. His partner was doing someone else's job and he was being left to work alone on the tasks she had actually been employed to do.

Except that she was only a step behind him by the time Hawk had conferred briefly with the scene commander and opened the back hatch of the squad car to get the equipment he needed. He picked up a digital camera and a can of spray paint.

'Have you spoken to the witness?'

'Not yet. There's pressure on to shift the wreck and get traffic flowing. I'm going to mark its position and get some photos before the tow truck moves in.' Hawk glanced up as the ambulance rolled past. The vehicle's beacons were flashing blue and red and its siren was activated as soon as it cleared the cordoned-off area. The noise was deafening for a moment and Hawk frowned.

'What's with the siren? That's not usual procedure for a return trip, is it?'

'It's a status-one patient. Post-arrest.' Charlotte told him. 'They need to get him to hospital as quickly as possible.'

'Is he going to survive?'

'I hope so,' Charlotte said quietly. 'His rhythm looked good and he was breathing spontaneously by the time he was loaded. We found his driver's licence,' she added. 'His name is Duncan Thomson. He's only forty-four.'

Only eight years older than Hawk. Suddenly the incident became more than a job. More than a scene of a traffic snarl-up and a major inconvenience for a large number of people trying to get to work. The strength of his own hope that the man would survive took Hawk by surprise. He didn't get emotionally involved with the victims of serious crashes. Never had. You couldn't afford to if you wanted to stay in this line of business for any length of time. Had the fact that he'd been more aware of what the paramedics were doing made the difference? If so, it could be another black mark to chalk up against having to work with Charlotte Laing.

Charlotte watched Hawk as he turned abruptly and strode towards the wreck. Her eyebrows rose as he walked straight past the man in the pinstripe suit, who was standing with a junior police officer. The witness still looked pale and shaken but he was clearly pulling himself together. Charlotte saw him look at his watch and then point to a sedan parked on the road's shoulder some distance uphill. Clearly, he wanted to leave the scene. Pulling a small notebook and pen from the pocket of her shirt, Charlotte also picked up a can of spray paint from the crate in the back of the squad car and moved purposefully.

'I'm Charlotte Laing,' she introduced herself to the witness, 'from the Serious Crash Squad. Thanks so much for waiting so long. Can you spare another minute or two to answer some questions for me?'

'Sure…I guess.' The man looked at his watch again. 'But I'm running awfully late for work.'

'It won't take long,' Charlotte promised. 'What's your name?'

'Andrew Duggan.'

'You did a great job, here, Andrew. It was you who made the triple-one call, wasn't it?'

The man nodded.

'And you started CPR?'

He nodded again. 'I did a first-aid course at work only last month.' His voice shook. 'I never thought I'd have to do it for real, though.'

'Pretty scary, isn't it?'

'Yeah.' Andrew rubbed a hand over his mouth as though reliving the mouth-to-mouth breathing. 'I'm going to carry one of those mask things from now on. Is he going to be all right, do you think?'

'He's very sick,' Charlotte responded seriously. 'But your actions gave him the best possible chance. He would definitely have died before anyone else got here if you hadn't started the CPR.'

'It took so long. By the time I realised there was something really wrong with him and called for an ambulance and found someone to help me get him out of the car…it seemed to take forever. And his face was all blue and… and…'

'I know.' Charlotte touched the man's arm in a sympathetic gesture. 'It's not nice. It sounds as though he might have collapsed even before the accident happened so there was nothing anyone could have done to help any earlier. You said you saw him slumped over the wheel?'

'Yes. I was in the inside lane.' Andrew pointed uphill. 'There was a car behind me in the middle lane and it was him leaning on his horn that made me notice the other car cutting in.'

'What speed were you doing, do you know?'

'Seventy-five, maybe 80 kph. The guy behind me slowed and I hit my brakes but I didn't need to. By the time he got into my lane he was going pretty fast. I thought he was just changing lanes. It wasn't until he kept going off the side of the road that I realised something was wrong. He hit the lamppost without even slowing down at all.'

'Can you show me where you were when you started braking?' Charlotte glanced over her shoulder to see Hawk's long frame bent over as he sprayed marks around the wrecked car's tyres. A tow truck was backing towards him. She continued making notes as she walked uphill with their witness.

One lane of traffic was now moving but Charlotte could identify tyre marks on the inside lane consistent with Andrew's braking manoeuvre. She also found marks in the middle lane that fitted the trajectory of an out-of-control vehicle that had ended its journey at the lamppost. She marked the areas with her can of bright orange spray paint.

Ten minutes later Charlotte had collected all the information she felt was needed from the witness.

'Thanks again,' she told Andrew as he waited to drive from the cordoned-off area into the line of still slowly moving traffic. 'You've been a great help. Are you sure you feel OK to go to work?'

Andrew nodded. 'I feel a lot better now.' He smiled at Charlotte. 'If I *did* do what you say a paramedic would have done under the same circumstances then maybe I should think about changing jobs.'

'I'd stick to supermarket managing if I were you.'
Charlotte grinned. 'Less stressful.'

'You'll call me, then? If you need to know anything
else?' He smiled again as Charlotte nodded. 'You could
call me anyway,' he suggested, 'if you fancy a drink or
something after work.'

'They're holding up the traffic for you.' Charlotte waved
Andrew away. 'Take care, now.' She turned, startled to find
Hawk standing right behind her.

'I was about to interview that guy.'

'I've done that.' Charlotte held up her notebook. 'I think
I've got everything we need.'

'Including his phone number?'

'Of course.' Charlotte didn't like the undertone. It was
normal procedure in any witness interview. If Hawk
thought she'd be following up any hint that the witness was
interested in social communication, then she was quite prepared to give him a piece of her mind regardless of their
situation.

Somewhat annoyingly, Hawk said nothing. He wasn't
even looking at Charlotte as his eyes focussed well past her
shoulder. 'What have you been marking?'

'Tyre marks. There's what looks like an acceleration
scuff at the start of the yaw. I assume the car's got automatic transmission?'

Hawk raised a single eyebrow. 'Why do you assume
that?'

'It fits,' Charlotte said calmly. 'If the driver collapsed he
could have had his foot depressing both the brake and the
accelerator. It would explain the mark and why his car's
speed kept increasing. Being slumped onto the steering-
wheel might also explain why the car travelled in a line
that took him across two lanes of traffic and straight into a
lamppost.'

Hawk's gaze suggested he was less than impressed with

Charlotte's line of reasoning. She raised an eyebrow right back at him. 'Do you have a problem with that scenario?'

'I have a problem with someone making a decision on the cause of a fatal crash before an investigation is complete.'

Charlotte raised her chin. 'Then let's get on with completing it, shall we?' She reached into the back of the squad car to remove one of the larger pieces of equipment but Hawk's movement was swifter.

'Here, I'll get that for you.'

Charlotte's glance was measured very deliberately. 'Thank you,' she said coolly, 'but I'm actually quite capable of lifting a theodolite all by myself.'

The hand retreated as though the tripod of the surveying gear was hot enough to have burnt him. 'Fine. I'll leave you to it, then.'

'Fine.' And Charlotte found herself watching Hawk's back as he strolled towards the other officers still on scene. Any sense of victory in asserting herself diminished rapidly as she found herself left alone to take measurements while Hawk engaged in what was clearly an enjoyable conversation with his colleagues. Judging by the frequent glances in her direction, Charlotte could be sure that she was providing the main topic of interest and she didn't like it. She was being assessed, and not only for her physical appearance or any impression of her personality Hawk might be passing on. She could bet that the occasional and very casual glances that came from the dark eyes of her new partner were taking account of exactly how well she was dealing with the task at hand.

Fortunately, it was a simple job. There was only one vehicle involved, the road was straight and there was no intersection. Permanent landmarks of trees and lampposts were ideally positioned to use as corners for her triangle and Charlotte's field sketch came together rapidly. She marked the direction of north, drew the road layout and documented the final position of the car involved in the crash. She showed the marks on the road and located the reference points for her triangle. The measurements were noted in metres and Charlotte also wrote quick notes on the weather, road and light conditions.

Traffic was flowing in two lanes by the time she finished thirty minutes later and the congestion was finally easing. The wrecked car had been removed and only one police car other than the SCS vehicle remained, its beacons flashing to warn oncoming motorists of the obstruction in the inside lane. Hawk was leaning on the side of his car, still talking to the other officers protecting the scene.

'So, he's got a job, then?' one was saying. 'That was quick.'

'It won't last,' Hawk responded darkly.

'What, the new job or the engagement?'

Charlotte guessed they were discussing Hawk's previous partner Cam. The man he didn't want her replacing. Had they been comparing her performance to what his would have been perhaps? Or teasing Hawk about having to work with a female colleague?

'Both, probably.'

Hawk's apparently pertinent comment to her unspoken thought was startling, but as Charlotte leaned into the car to stow the theodolite she realised that the comment was referring to the permanence of Cam's new interests. She straightened.

'Is Cam likely to change his mind, then?' She smiled sweetly at the three male officers. 'And there I was thinking that was a *woman's* prerogative.'

Hawk showed no reaction to the meaningful glances his colleagues bestowed upon him but his eyes narrowed as he slid behind the wheel of his car. So, that plump paramedic had repeated what he'd said to her friend, had she? That figured. You couldn't trust a woman to keep her mouth shut. He'd have to be very careful what he said in future.

He'd spent less than two hours in this woman's company and Hawk already had the uncomfortable feeling that working with her, even temporarily, was going to be more of a challenge than he'd anticipated. So far, the opportunities to try and establish control appeared to have backfired in some mysterious manner. Hawk was silent throughout the journey back to Headquarters. Another opportunity was bound to present itself and he needed to be ready for it. If ground rules were being set, then he intended to be the one to put them in place.

Charlotte used her lunch-break to collect the last item of her personal work supplies from her hatchback in the building's basement car park. She also took the time to try calling Laura on her mobile phone.

'You busy?'

'No, we're just heading back to station for lunch. We just took a kid with febrile convulsions into Emergency.'

'How did it go with our car-accident victim this morning?'

'Fantastic result! He was in normal sinus rhythm by the time we reached Emergency. He's woken up since and has a bit of short-term memory loss but that's all.'

'Any evidence of an MI?'

'No. They're thinking the collapse might have been rhythm related. Long QT syndrome maybe. He's lined up for electro-physiology testing in the next day or two.'

'He's been lucky.'

'I'll say. It was also lucky he didn't have his family in the car or involve any other vehicles.'

'Made my job easier,' Charlotte said wryly. 'Which was just as well seeing as I was under a performance review.' She sighed. 'We probably won't need any of it, anyway, seeing as it's not a fatal. All that stress for nothing.'

'How's it going with the hawk?'

'Interesting.' Charlotte found herself smiling. 'Bit of a power play so far. Would you believe he holds doors open for me? And offers to lift heavy stuff?'

'That's very gentlemanly.'

'I think it's intended to be more of a put-down,' Charlotte countered. 'But don't worry. I got to one door first when he was showing me around so I held it open for him.'

Laura chuckled. 'You sound like you're enjoying it. What's your office like?'

'OK. It's got everything we need. Bit on the small side.'

'I'd reckon something the size of a football field would be on the small side with that man sharing it.'

Charlotte grinned. 'We'll sort it out. I think we're due for a showdown of some sort before the day's out and I might have just the thing to set it off.'

'What's that?'

'My paramedic kit. I'm about to lug it upstairs and let him know we need to find room for it in an already over-stuffed squad car. It should open that can of worms fairly effectively.'

It did.

Hawk eyed the large modified backpack that Charlotte carried into the office as though it were an unexploded bomb.

'What the hell is that?'

'My paramedic kit,' Charlotte replied calmly. 'Lance Currie told me he'd let you know that I was authorised to carry it in our squad car.'

'You could go camping for a week with a pack that size.'

'I carry full intubation gear, cervical collars, IV supplies and fluid. Also a range of drugs, a Hare traction splint and a small oxygen cylinder. Basis equipment for resuscitation and stabilisation of a severely injured accident victim.'

'Even I know that splinting something isn't a priority in a life-threatening situation.' Hawk's resolve not to show his ignorance in medical matters had deserted him. 'Whatever that rabbity thing is, it's probably taking up unnecessary space.'

Charlotte tried to control the twitch of her lips but wasn't entirely successful. 'A Hare traction splint is used for a broken femur. It helps control bleeding. Blood loss from a long bone fracture can be as much as a litre. If that's added to blood loss from other injuries, it can stack up to fatal hypovolaemic shock in a short space of time. Any blood loss needs to be addressed as quickly as possible.'

Hawk hated being in no position to argue. 'We share a squad car, not an ambulance. If carrying all your luggage interferes with me being able to do my job then it's gone.'

'What's your problem here, Owen? Finding room for my "luggage" or me being a paramedic as well as a crash investigator?'

'Trying to do two jobs at the same time,' Hawk snapped. 'What's probably going to happen is that I'll end up doing the job you've been employed for while you're fluffing around on scene, sticking needles into people.'

'Like I did this morning?' Charlotte made an incredulous huffing sound that filled Hawk's silence. She wasn't about to be intimidated by his aggressively prolonged eye contact either. She stared right back at him. 'And did you really say *fluffing*?'

Hawk broke the eye contact and glared at the offending kit instead. 'We have enough to do on scene without distractions. OK, you didn't get so involved this morning because there was already an ambulance on scene. What happens if we get somewhere first? How can you possibly give this job the concentration it has to have if you're dealing with patients?' He was being unfair, he knew that, but this was the opportunity. Or he'd thought it was. Now he wasn't so sure but he couldn't afford to back down.

'I "deal" with patients only if there's no other medical assistance available or when my qualifications allow me to assist a crew that might not include someone with my level of qualifications. My input is limited to the point where victims are transported to hospital.' Charlotte was clearly making an effort to maintain a tone of reason. 'The preservation of life and the safety of everybody on scene is the first priority for any emergency service personnel arriving at any incident. Or would you disagree?'

Hawk was losing here, he could sense it. The sensible thing to do would be to retreat with as much dignity as possible.

'I can hardly disagree with a blanket statement that all emergency services embrace. What I'm talking about is interference with a specific set of protocols that apply to the SCS. To *me*.'

'Look, I understand your concern.' Maybe Charlotte had the grace to allow a dignified retreat now that she had won yet another unspoken challenge on their private agendas. 'Being involved for any length of time with patient care is not a situation that is going to arise very frequently, and when it does it can actually aid an investigation.'

'Oh?'

'Patients say things. Injuries can tell their own stories. You can notice a lot of small details coming at a scene from a slightly different perspective. The time that might be lost on scene is made up for later when we don't have to interview the ambulance crew or try and extract patient details from hospital staff. The contacts I have with the hospital can also be useful.'

Dammit. What she said made perfect sense but Hawk wasn't about to make her feel appreciated for the extra dimension she could bring to the SCS.

'Let's just see how it goes,' Charlotte continued. 'I'm happy to discuss any issues at any time. If you have any problems with the way I do this job, I would like to hear about them. From you,' she added. 'Not through some staff grapevine.'

'Don't worry,' Hawk responded curtly. 'You will.' He turned abruptly back to his computer screen, where producing the scene map for a fatal crash from the previous week awaited him.

Charlotte busied herself sorting out her desk, thankful for the respite turning her back on her new colleague provided. She was still very aware of him sitting less than six feet away from her, however. Laura was right. He could be sitting at the end of a football field and his presence would still be noticeable. His aura crowded the small area and the empty surface of her own desk was a tiny space to claim as her own. How long would it take before she stopped feeling like an unwelcome intruder?

At least other people were willing to make her feel welcome. Officers from other departments who had known Charlotte from her early career in the police force dropped in to say hello during the course of the afternoon.

'It's so good to see you again, Charlie. I hope you're here to stay this time.'

'Sure am.' Charlotte ignored the vibes concerning the temporary nature of her appointment that were coming from the other side of the room. 'I love this job.'

The fact that Charlotte had placed a small picture in a heart-shaped frame on her desk made it inevitable that one of her visitors would mention Jamie.

'I'm sorry I never made it to the funeral.'

'It's OK. It was a long way for you and it's a long time ago now.'

'I was really sorry to hear about it. Did you get my letter?'

'Yes, I did. Thanks.'

'You guys were so perfect for each other.'

'Yeah.' The vibes coming from Hawk were different

now. And he had turned his head just far enough to demonstrate the fact that he was eavesdropping.

Charlotte said nothing more. There was no way they were going to cover any personal ground until they had sorted out some professional boundaries. Especially any related to her gender. The assessing glances her body was receiving from male officers, including Owen Hawkins, were far more unwelcome than Hawk found her paramedic qualifications to be. And he'd had his chance to air his resentment. Charlotte was waiting for her turn.

It came, in the final minutes of her first day on the job, when she was about to pack up and go home. Other staff members were also heading home and one poked his head into the office.

'Hey, Hawk. Fancy a beer after work?'

'I'm on call tonight, Murphy. Another night would be great.'

'You're always on call, mate.'

'I'll get some time off for good behaviour soon. My new colleague and I will be sharing the on-call duties as soon as she's settled in a bit.'

Murphy's eyes widened as Charlotte turned. He grinned at Hawk and lowered his voice. 'This is your new colleague? You lucky, lucky guy.'

'That remains to be seen,' Hawk responded just as quietly. Then he spoke more loudly. 'Charlotte, this is Greg Murphy, one of our detectives.'

'Hi, Greg.' Charlotte gave him only the briefest smile. So Hawk was waiting to see if he'd get 'lucky' was he? He should learn to lower his voice more effectively.

'Would *you* like to come out for a beer?' Murphy was still grinning. Or was it leering? 'I would consider it rude not to welcome a new colleague with a celebratory drink.'

'No, thanks.' Charlotte didn't bother expanding on her decision. She fitted the folder of local scene protocols into her shoulder-bag. She had every intention of reading them thoroughly before arriving at work in the morning.

'I need to finish this,' Hawk was telling Murphy. 'Catch you later?'

'Sure.' Murphy wasn't offended by the brush-off. He leaned a little further through the doorway. 'I'm surprised you're getting any work done, mate,' he said cheerfully. 'Just as well Charlotte's not blonde, eh?'

Instead of following Murphy out of the office, Charlotte closed the door and turned back to face Hawk.

'What was that about?'

He looked up at the new interruption with a weary expression. 'What?'

'Why is it just as well I'm not blonde?'

Hawk shrugged. 'I have no idea. Maybe Murphy has a thing about blondes.'

Charlotte gave him a long-suffering look. She wasn't about to let him think he could get away with treating her like an idiot. And she certainly wasn't about to let him think that sexual harassment was tolerable. Either the blatant kind that Greg Murphy displayed or the subtle inferences Hawk had been providing.

'Murphy must be an extremely shallow person, then. I hope that any blonde unfortunate enough to have him hitting on her finds out sooner rather than later.'

'I wouldn't worry about it. You're safe.'

'By virtue of not being blonde?' Charlotte's words dripped acid. 'Listen, Owen, I want to get something straight here, and I may as well do it on my first day. I'm not about to tolerate getting hit on by anyone I work with. Feel free to pass it on.'

'I'm sure word will get around fast enough.'

'I'm hardly breaking new ground.' Charlotte shook her head. 'I'm far from the first woman to join the police force. Why am I getting the impression that I've stepped into some boys' only club?'

'You're the first woman to join the SCS. Here, anyway.'

'I'm here to do a job. The fact that I'm female has nothing to do with it.'

'You're new. Everyone has to prove themselves. Respect is something that's earned.'

'That cuts both ways.' Charlotte's tone was intended to be a warning. 'And I'm not going to have any respect for a colleague who assumes I'm more interested in having sex than doing my job.'

'At least we have something in common, then.' The hint of a smile made Charlotte realise it was the first she had received. In fact, had she even seen him smile at anyone else during the course of today?

'And that is?'

'Not letting personal relationships interfere with a career.'

'So you'll stop looking at me as if I'm parading around in my underwear, then?'

Hawk's jaw dropped. 'I haven't been!'

'Yes, you have,' Charlotte contradicted. 'And so has every other male I've met so far today. I'm getting assessed and that assessment is being based purely on what I look like.'

'You're not exactly what any of us expected, you know.'

'You mean I'm not short, fat and ugly? Hell bent on a tough career in the police force because I'm too much of a dog to catch myself a husband?'

Hawk's laughter was as astonishing as the way his amusement changed his face. Charlotte had been wondering if she'd even seen him smile and now she had elicited a bark of rich sound and a smile that made him look like a stranger all over again. The fierce lines of his face hadn't changed but any hint of arrogance or aggression had evaporated, at least for the moment. In fact, the gleam in those dark blue eyes confirmed that Charlotte had hit the nail

squarely on the head and that her perception was both unexpected and quite admirable.

'Don't worry.' The faintly embarrassed undertone to
Hawk's voice as he turned back to his computer gave away
the fact that he had shared the general expectation of what
she would be like. 'I can't guarantee you won't be hit on,'
he continued. 'But I can assure you it won't be by me. I've
never slept with a partner and I don't intend to start now.'

'Your partners have always been men.'

'So?' Hawk turned to face Charlotte again and she held
his gaze. A gaze that might just hold the tiniest amount of
respect for the way she had confronted this issue.

He also seemed to be telling her that he wasn't going to
let the fact that she was female make any difference to their
professional relationship. She smiled slowly.

'I think we understand each other…Hawk.' The use of
his nickname was only a shade tentative.

'I'm sure we do…Charlie.' Hawk's smile acknowledged
the new space they were entering.

As colleagues.

CHAPTER THREE

'YOU *bastard*!'

Charlotte's head turned sharply at the raw anger in the statement from the rapidly approaching stranger.

'There's a dead woman in that car and it's *your* fault!'

'I didn't even see her!'

'You shouldn't be allowed on the road. You're a useless, incompetent—'

'Excuse *me*.' Charlotte turned her body and stepped sideways into the path of the stranger. 'Who are you?'

'I work in those offices.' The man jerked an arm in the direction of a building over the road. 'I saw the whole thing.'

'Then we'll certainly take your statement,' Charlotte told him calmly. 'If you go and wait beside that police car over there, I'll—'

'He just turned this bloody great truck in front of her. She didn't stand a chance. *Look* at her, you moron!'

Unfortunately, it was still possible to see the mangled body in the driver's seat of the small hatchback. The fire officers were trying to position a tarpaulin as a shield prior to cutting the woman's body free from the wreck, but it was proving difficult. Wellington wasn't known as the 'windy city' for nothing.

'She was probably on her way to pick her kids up from school.' The witness was clearly becoming even more upset at the closer view he was now getting of the disastrous aftermath of the accident, but his reaction paled in comparison to the man he was confronting. The driver of the truck involved was shaking visibly beneath the blanket an ambulance officer had draped over his shoulders. Now he had tears coursing down his face.

'I've got kids myself,' he said brokenly. 'Oh...*God*! What have I *done*?'

'I'll tell you exactly what you've done, you damned—' The witness shoved Charlotte aside and she stumbled sideways, but he didn't get as far as the truck driver because another figure slipped smoothly into his path.

'*Move*,' Hawk snapped. 'If you're not behind that police cordon in ten seconds, I'll have you arrested, mate.'

The man blinked, his fury hijacked by a dawning recognition that he no longer had any chance to control this situation. Charlotte was wearing a rather similarly stunned expression. In the two weeks she had been working with Owen Hawkins she had tucked away the impression that she would not want to face his anger. Now she was seeing it for the first time and she could confirm that impression. With bells on.

Hawk often looked focussed, uncompromising and even fiercely determined, but right now his expression was calmly murderous. The man he was facing outweighed him considerably and was in a charged emotional state that could readily be expressed in physical violence, but Hawk's expression and tone had been enough to stop him as effectively as a stone wall.

'And don't...*ever*...touch a police officer again.' The words dripped like ice into the sudden silence. 'Unless you want to be arrested for assault.'

'But...I saw it.'

'Officer Jackson will take your statement. Over *there*.'

'OK...sure.' The man turned and almost stumbled in his newfound eagerness to co-operate. Charlotte could sympathise with his bemusement. She was still feeling stunned herself. Not so much by the ease with which Hawk had defused the potentially dangerous situation but by the fact that his anger had been harnessed to protect her.

She wouldn't have considered she needed that kind of protection. She should be as annoyed about it as she had been to have doors held open for her or offers to have heavy objects lifted on her behalf. She had been in more than one dodgy situation as both a crash investigator and a paramedic and she had been quite capable of looking after herself. Determined to, in fact. Jamie's death had bred the determination to cope alone both personally and professionally. The force of that unexpected shove had been alarming, however, and to have that kind of back-up available from a partner was reassuring. Welcome, even.

The second or two of silence was shattered as the pneumatic cutting gear the fire service needed kicked into action. Another sound also managed to reach the trio of figures that included Charlotte.

'Daddy! *Daddy!*'

She hadn't expected the presence of the small boy who was being lifted from the back of the ambulance parked close by. He looked to be about four years old and was making a beeline for the truck driver.

'Is he OK?'

An ambulance officer followed in the child's wake. 'He's fine. How are you doing now?'

'I'm fine.' The truck driver reached down to take his son in his arms but he was struggling for control as he looked up at Hawk.

'I didn't even see her. The road was clear when I started the turn. I'm sure it was. And then I checked again and there she was...' He caught a ragged breath. 'I put my foot down. I thought she had time to stop but that I'd better get out of the way fast just in case. And then I heard it hit and...and...' Racking sobs broke his speech and he buried his face against his son's shoulder.

'It's OK,' Charlotte found herself saying as she put her hand on his arm. 'Come and sit down for a minute.'

It took some time to get a statement from the distraught truck driver, Steve Poulsen. He knew he could lose his job and he had four children to support. It had also been the first time he'd given his son, Ben, the treat of having a day on the road with him, but the relief that his child was unhurt or the worry about losing his livelihood couldn't begin to mitigate the grief that a life had been lost and that it could have been his fault. Charlotte spent nearly an hour talking to Steve before arranging a squad car to take him home.

Hawk was marking the scene and taking photographs. Charlotte joined him and they spent another hour working together as the scene was gradually cleared. The ambulance was long gone, not having been needed for Steve or Ben and unable to do anything for the woman in the car. A hearse arrived and left with the victim's body and then the fire appliances departed. A tow truck took the wrecked car away and the truck was driven away to be impounded for further forensic investigation. By the time Hawk and Charlotte had collected the information they needed, broken glass was being swept from the road and the spectators were finally dispersing, leaving only the SCS and one other police vehicle present. One of the officers from that car approached Hawk.

'Are you guys nearly done?'

'Nearly.'

'There's a call out to any available vehicles for an armed robbery in town.' Young Officer Jackson looked eager to get in on the action.

'You go,' Hawk told him. 'We'll close the scene here.'

'I'm supposed to go and see the dead woman's family and break the news.' Jackson looked far less keen for that unpleasant duty.

'Have you got her details?'

'Yeah.' A page of his notebook and a driver's licence were located and Jackson looked hopeful. He ripped the page out as Hawk extended his hand.

'Are you sure? Hey, thanks, Hawk. I owe you one.'

'No problem.'

Charlotte watched as Jackson flicked on his squad car's beacons and then started the siren as soon as the car was rolling.

'That was a nice thing to do.'

'Not really.' Hawk was folding the legs of the theodolite's tripod. 'It could be useful for us to talk to her family anyway. I'd like to know what her state of mind was.'

Charlotte nodded. 'It's a bit weird, isn't it, not having any braking marks further up the hill? Either she just wasn't looking or the truck *did* turn directly into her path.'

Hawk looked from the point the truck had turned across the road into the driveway up to the bend in the road some distance uphill. 'The speedo's locked at 70 kph, which is the speed limit here. It could be that there isn't enough stopping distance from that bend even if the road was clear when he started his turn.'

It was exactly the kind of information the SCS could establish, report to the appropriate authorities and have a change made that could make the road safer for future drivers.

'We'll need to do some testing,' Charlotte said. 'Skid testing for speed and stopping time and for the truck turning. How long does it take, do you think, to turn a truck that size across half the road width?'

'I'd guess somewhere between five and eight seconds, but it would only be a guess.'

Charlotte wasn't so sure about that. Hawk's ability to calculate time and distances had impressed her considerably over the last two weeks. She relied on her computer programs to supply many of the results from the complicated equations they needed to use in their investigations. Owen Hawkins seemed quite capable of doing most of them in his head, which was irritating. Had Cam been just as clever mathematically? She had no hope of competing with a skill like that.

She moved to pick up the cones protecting their work space. 'We'll need to check out those advertising hoardings on the roadside. It could be that they're obstructing visibility.' It was another aspect of the scene's environment that would be easy enough to correct if an influence was proved.

A few minutes later, Charlotte started the car. 'Where are we headed?' she queried.

'Breakwater Bay. It's a few kilometres up the coast.'

'What information have we got?'

'Her name's Katrina Jones. Thirty-four years old. Next of kin are listed as her parents—at the same address.'

'I guess her parents might be in their sixties,' Charlotte said, 'so it's quite likely we'll find someone at home.' It seemed unusual for someone Katrina's age to be living at home. Had she been single? Or had she moved home for help in coping as a solo mother? She hoped there were no children involved. Breaking this kind of news was always worse when the victim was a parent of young children.

Katrina Jones had not been a mother but her parents were devastated at the information Charlotte and Hawk had to impart.

'But she's such a careful driver. Trina's never had an accident.' Her father had slumped into a chair, his face grey.

His wife was pale. Numbed by the shock, she was desperately trying to avoid facing reality. 'You must have made a mistake. Maybe someone stole her car.'

'We have her driver's licence, Mrs Jones. From her handbag.'

'They might have stolen the car *and* the handbag.'

'No.' Charlotte had looked at the photo ID on the licence. While the victim's face had been virtually unrecognisable, there could be no mistake with the distinctively long, blond hair. 'I'm terribly sorry but there hasn't been a mistake. Your daughter has died as the result of the crash.'

She looked from Katrina's mother to the grey-faced man in the armchair. She hated this part of a police officer's job. As a paramedic it never seemed quite this awful. At least she would have been seen to have done something to try and help prior to announcing such devastating news. Charlotte swallowed hard. 'I'm terribly sorry,' she repeated.

Katrina's father had his head bowed. Charlotte could see beads of perspiration appearing where his hairline had receded. She stepped closer.

'Are you all right, Mr Jones?'

Charlotte caught the ironic glance she received from Hawk. The message was crystal clear. Of course he wasn't all right. He'd just been told his only daughter was dead. Charlotte ignored the look and crouched beside the armchair. It was an automatic gesture to pick up the man's wrist and feel for a pulse.

'He's got a bad heart.' Mrs Jones latched onto the potential distraction. 'He had triple bypass surgery only last year.' She clutched at her husband's other hand. 'Stan? Are you all right, love?'

'Do you have any chest pain at the moment?' Charlotte didn't like the erratic rhythm her fingers detected. Frequent missed beats could herald a medical emergency.

Stan Jones nodded slowly. His eyes were closed and tears trickled down to join the perspiration on his face. His colour was awful and Charlotte noted the increasing effort he was making to draw breath. She glanced up at Hawk.

'Could you get my kit from the car, please, Hawk?' Her query was calm but Hawk's nod showed his instant comprehension of the actual message her gaze was delivering. 'Perhaps you could call for an ambulance as well.'

Mrs Jones gaped. 'Oh...dear! Do you think it's that bad?'

'Let's just be on the safe side.'

Charlotte's words to Mrs Jones had been reassuring but Hawk moved rapidly. He called through to the control centre on the squad car radio.

'Can we have an ambulance to this address?'

'Nature of call?'

'There's a paramedic with the man and she thinks he needs one. He could be having a heart attack, I guess.'

'Is it urgent?'

Hawk remembered the alarm he had detected in the depths of Charlotte's quick glance despite the calm tone of her voice. 'Yes,' he said decisively. 'It's urgent.'

Pulling the bulky kit from the back of the car, Hawk hoped his assessment had been correct. Walking back into the living room of the Joneses' house, he wished he had been wrong.

Stan was slumped forward. Charlotte had her arms under his shoulders and was pulling him from the chair.

'Help me get him onto the floor, Hawk.'

Mrs Jones was in the way. Hawk put a hand on each of her shoulders and moved her firmly but gently to one side. She resisted.

'Stan! Stan, what's the matter with you?'

'It's all right, Mrs Jones,' Hawk said. 'Charlie here is a paramedic. She'll know how to help Stan.' Hoping like hell this statement was correct, Hawk moved even more swiftly, picking up Stan's legs and helping Charlotte place him face up on the incongruously cheerful floral carpet.

Charlotte checked his mouth briefly, then tilted his head back. She put one ear close to his mouth and nose, one hand resting on his diaphragm. 'He's not breathing,' she told Hawk quietly. 'Can you open my kit, please, Hawk? You'll find a mask with a soft bag that looks like a rugby ball attached to it.'

She had her hand on Stan's neck now, feeling for a carotid pulse. Hawk saw the imperceptible shake of her head and the way her lips set into a determined line. He didn't mind that she was describing her equipment in terms a three-year-old might understand. This was serious and he was way out of his comfort zone.

Charlotte took the ambubag from Hawk, held the mask firmly on Stan's face and pressed the bag. His chest rose and fell. She gave him another breath and glanced up at Hawk. 'Do you know how to do chest compressions?'

'Kind of.' Hawk's mouth felt suddenly dry. 'I did a first-aid course.' The thought of doing it for real was terrifying. No wonder the bystander at that first crash they had attended together had looked so shaken. Somebody's life might depend on his input here. 'It's a few years ago, though.'

'Look.' Charlotte was using some heavy-duty scissors to cut Stan's clothing. A woollen jersey, plaid shirt and a singlet separated to reveal his chest. 'Here's the bottom rib.' She ran her fingers up the prominent curve on the skinny chest. 'Go to the sternal notch in the middle here and then measure two finger widths up. Place the heel of your other hand at that point, then lace the fingers of both hands together. Like this.'

The demonstration was as swift and smooth as her speech. 'Straighten your arms and lean forward. You need to press hard enough to reach a depth of three to five centimetres and it needs to be this fast.' The compressions were far more rapid than Hawk would have thought necessary.

'Count…silently,' Charlotte advised Hawk as she moved

aside, indicating her expectation that he would take over. 'Every fifteen compressions, pause, and I'll get a couple of breaths into him.'

Hawk knelt beside Charlotte, his thigh pressing against hers for a few moments as she watched to make sure he remembered her directions. He didn't notice the tiny shake in his hand as he traced the line of the bottom rib and positioned his hands. He started compressions, taken aback by how different a human felt to the plastic dummy he vaguely remembered from the first-aid course. He concentrated hard.

'Good. You're doing well, Hawk. Don't forget to count.' Charlotte was pulling equipment from her kit. She attached a small oxygen cylinder to the bag mask for the next two breaths she gave Stan, but the next time Hawk paused she was ready for a more complicated manoeuvre. She had a silver instrument in her hand and a tube lying on top of its opened sterile packaging beside her.

'I'll get you to press on Stan's Adam's apple for a second here, Hawk.' Charlotte had levered Stan's mouth open with the blade of the laryngoscope and was peering in as she inserted the tube. 'It helps me visualise the vocal cords and get this endotracheal tube positioned correctly.'

It took only seconds to complete the intubation and Hawk had to trace Stan's ribs again to find his hand position and restart the compressions. Charlotte had attached the bag mask and oxygen to the tube protecting Stan's airway by the time he was due for another two breaths and then her hands were into the kit again, pulling IV gear out.

'Where's your defibrillator?' Hawk was pleased he'd remembered the name of the life-saving cardiac equipment. This man's heart had stopped and it was clearly what they needed right now.

'I don't carry one. We'll have to keep up the CPR until we get back-up.'

Hawk bent to his task again but a sense of hopelessness was creeping in. She had a miniature oxygen cylinder in her pack. Surely it was big enough to hold a small version of a defibrillator? The physical effort involved was making itself apparent now as well. This was hard work and they were some distance from the city. How long would it take for an ambulance to arrive? Trying to reassess the depth of his compressions, Hawk pressed a little harder on Stan's chest. To his horror he felt something crunching under the heel of his hand. His gaze flew up to meet Charlotte's. She continued attaching the tourniquet to Stan's arm but her brief glance was reassuring.

'It was just a rib,' she murmured. 'It happens. You're doing just fine, Hawk.'

And suddenly Hawk didn't feel tired or hopeless any more. He was proud of what he was doing to help and he was proud to be with Charlotte who clearly knew what she was doing. Having inserted an IV line into Stan's arm, she then startled Hawk by turning to speak to Mrs Jones. He'd been focussed enough to forget he wasn't alone with Charlotte and their patient. He glanced up to see Stan's wife perched on the arm of her husband's chair; her hands clasped and pressed against her mouth, her eyes wide and terrified.

'We're doing all we can to help Stan,' Charlotte told her quietly.

'Wh-what's happening?'

'His heart has stopped. What we're doing is helping him breathe and keeping his circulation going until some more help arrives.'

'Is...is he going to be all right?'

'He's very sick,' Charlotte said carefully. 'But we're not going to give up just yet. Can you go and make sure the front door is open? The ambulance shouldn't be too far away now.'

It was further away than Hawk would have wished. The contact with Mrs Jones had reminded him of why they were in this situation in the first place. This woman had just been informed that she had lost her daughter. And now her husband was possibly dying right in front of her. The relief that the arrival of the ambulance crew and all their gear engendered was almost enough to make Hawk feel light-headed. He moved aside as an ambulance officer took over compressions and another slapped electrodes and gel pads to Stan's chest.

'Extensive cardiac history,' Charlotte told the paramedic in charge of the crew. 'Sudden collapse after being informed of the death of his daughter in an MVA.'

The paramedic swore under his breath and shook his head, but his gaze was fixed on the screen of the life pack. He caught Charlotte's gaze. 'What do you reckon?' he queried. 'Fine VF?'

Charlotte's expression was grim. 'Barely more than asystole.'

'Worth a shot?'

Charlotte nodded. She rocked back on her heels as the paramedic called for a clear space. Hawk stepped further back as he watched the convulsive jerk.

'It's asystole now.'

'Let's get some adrenaline on board.'

'Sure. Oh, great—you've already got an IV in.'

Hawk looked away from the rapid actions of the paramedics as they continued CPR and started drawing up and administering drugs. His gaze found Mrs Jones, back in her position by the armchair but looking as though she herself might fall over any second. Hawk moved. At least there was something useful he could still do. He put his arm around the older woman and encouraged her to turn away.

'Come with me,' he said gently. 'I think we should give the experts a bit of space for a minute.' He led Mrs Jones towards the kitchen. 'They're doing everything they can for Stan.'

'But that's a police officer,' Mrs Jones said anxiously. 'How does she know what to do?'

'She's a rather special police officer,' Hawk heard himself say. He hoped the emergency personnel behind them were too preoccupied to overhear his reassuring statement. 'She's a paramedic as well.'

If Charlotte had overheard the remark she gave no indication of it and any new appreciation Hawk might have for her diverse talents were buried over the next few days by the heavy workload the team was under. The victory Charlotte felt in finally persuading Hawk to take the time to accompany her to the Joneses' funeral service was dampened by his obvious discomfort in being there. He was still looking less than happy when they had left as soon as could be considered courteous.

'We shouldn't have gone. It was an intrusion.'

'I don't think so.' Charlotte felt the gears change as she accelerated in their departure from the funeral home car park. 'It's not as if we're going to the graveside ceremony. We were simply paying our respects to the family of a case we're involved in.'

She glanced at Hawk's profile after a minute's silence. 'I know how you feel,' she offered. 'I used to feel the same way but Jamie persuaded me. He always attended the funerals associated with his cases and he convinced me that the benefits outweighed the less pleasant aspects.'

The grunt Hawk made suggested he was not likely to be easily swayed. 'I don't see how.'

'He reckoned it gave a more personal connection to a case.'

'That's not something *I* would consider a good thing. If we get too involved, we can't do our jobs properly.'

'More open communication with other people involved, like relatives and friends, *can* be a good thing, though. Besides, you can't argue that it doesn't give a more human element to our job.' Charlotte expelled her breath in a huff that could have signified mirth. 'On second thoughts, I'd guess that you could argue about anything. So feel free, Hawk. Tell me I'm barking up the wrong tree or something.'

'I wouldn't dream of it,' Hawk said pleasantly. 'Far be it from me to contradict any wisdom you inherited from Jamie.'

Silence fell again in the car and Charlotte gritted her teeth. OK, maybe she *did* mention Jamie quite often but Hawk was just being immature if he let it get up his nose. It was tit for tat, anyway. He talked about Cam just as often. And Charlotte couldn't help making comparisons. That disturbing level of awareness she had of Hawk, both physically and professionally, had made her inward comparisons an almost automatic habit by now. And three weeks of close professional contact with Owen Hawkins had highlighted huge differences between the two men. The example of Hawk's reaction to attending the funeral had been another biggie.

Jamie wouldn't have thought of doing otherwise but then, he had been a people person. Enormously popular, he'd been able to establish an instant and lasting bond with virtually everyone he'd met. He had been laid back to the point where simply his presence had lightened an atmosphere and generated good humour and laughter.

So much laughter. Charlotte had fallen in love with him because of the way he'd always been able to make her laugh, no matter how bad she'd been feeling. If it had been Jamie sitting beside her in the car now, he would probably have found something to make her laugh even in the wake of attending the tragic double funeral of the whole of Eileen

Jones's immediate family. She stole another sideways glance at Hawk. Almost an accusatory glare that he couldn't be more like Jamie.

Her passenger was massaging his forehead between the thumb and fingers of one hand and Charlotte's resentment faded.

'Have you got a headache?'

'No.'

They lapsed into yet another silence as Charlotte tried to concentrate on the route she was taking. She had to stop comparing Hawk to Jamie. It wasn't fair on Hawk and it wasn't helping her to settle into this new job. There was no comparison anyway. The two men were simply too different. The thought of describing Hawk as laid back would make Laura hoot with laughter and Charlotte would concur. There was an intensity about Owen Hawkins that made him capable of generating tension without even trying.

And Charlotte could probably count on the fingers of one hand the number of times she'd seen him really smile. Aloof, that was the word for it. She didn't believe it was because he didn't have a sense of humour or that he lacked compassion. He was probably just very careful about who he let close enough to share it.

It was Hawk that broke this silence. 'Bit rough, wasn't it?' he said quietly. 'She's lost her whole family.'

'Yeah.' Maybe he wasn't so aloof at the moment. That head-rubbing gesture might have signified an emotional reaction deeper than Charlotte had credited. Or maybe he had decided to let Charlotte a little closer. The amount of pleasure the thought gave was not warranted, however, and it wasn't welcome. Charlotte flicked on her indicator and checked her rear-view mirror, effectively excusing any further comment. She did not crave Owen Hawkins's acceptance on anything more than a professional level.

'At least that truck driver didn't turn up. He said he was going to, didn't he?'

'He was very upset at the time.' Charlotte began to slow the car as she checked house numbers on letterboxes. 'I scheduled this interview so he wouldn't have the chance to attend, though, just in case. I didn't think his presence would have helped anyone—including him.'

'It's been a week. He should be pulling himself together by now.'

Charlotte decided she might need to revise her opinion of Hawk's level of compassion. 'He's lost his job and he has a court appearance pending. It must be pretty tough when you've got four young children to support.'

'Let's hope he feels more communicative than he did the last time we tried to talk to him.'

Steve Poulsen was, in fact, nowhere to be seen when Hawk and Charlotte knocked at the door of his modest house in an outlying suburb of Wellington.

'He's still in bed.' Steve's wife, Jane, looked embarrassed but Charlotte could see her underlying distress. 'He won't get up. He says there's no point.'

They ended up talking to Jane in the tiny kitchen, with Ben and another pre-schooler playing nearby and a baby in a high-chair banging a half-chewed rusk on the tray.

'He sounds very depressed,' Charlotte said when Jane had let her worries flood out. 'Has he seen his doctor?'

'He won't.' Jane shook her head unhappily. 'He doesn't want to talk to anyone.' Tears began flowing again. 'He says…he says he's a murderer and he can't live with knowing that.'

The baby started howling in sympathy with his distressed mother and Jane reached to pick the infant up. 'I don't believe it could have been Steve's fault,' she said brokenly. 'He's just so careful.'

Charlotte waited until she was back in the car with Hawk to announce her decision.

'I'm going to take another look at this job. If there's some way of clearing Steve, I want to find it.'

'We've completed the investigation.'

'That witness from the office block isn't reliable. He decided Steve was at fault and that was that. He couldn't even see the bend from his window so he can't know whether Katrina's car was visible when Steve started his turn.'

'She wasn't speeding. The line of vision wasn't obscured by the hoardings. There was nothing wrong with her car. If the road had been clear when he started his turn, there was no reason she couldn't have had time to stop.'

Charlotte was silent. They had spent hours over the last week conducting the tests. They had done skid tests in a car similar to Katrina's and measured the friction marks to confirm her speed as being within the limit. They had used a truck to measure turning times and Hawk had been as close as she had suspected he would be in his estimation. It took between 4.6 and 6.3 seconds for the turn. They had measured the visibility distance to the bend at the start of the turn. Eighty-two metres. They had made a scale plan for sight lines. A car travelling at 70 kph would have taken just over four seconds to cover the distance. Less than the time for the turn but plenty of time to stop if the brakes had been applied earlier.

Why hadn't Katrina seen the truck? The obvious answer was that Steve had miscalculated the time he would need for his turn or that he had not seen the car, but Charlotte wasn't content to leave it.

'Has Katrina's cellphone been returned to her mother?'

'Not that I know of. But I checked it. There were no recent calls at the time of the accident so she wasn't speaking to anyone. No missed calls either, so she wasn't trying to pick it up off the floor or anything.'

'I'd like to take a look at it.'

'Why?' Hawk's tone challenged her to accuse him of missing something and Charlotte sighed. It was about time they stopped watching how each other did their jobs, looking for something to criticise or feel offended about. She wasn't trying to catch him out here or prove anything. She just wanted to solve the case to her own satisfaction.

'I'm not sure,' she confessed. 'I just have the feeling we might be missing something.'

'Feminine intuition?' Hawk snorted softly and Charlotte gave him a somewhat scathing glance. She decided against sharing the odd comment Katrina's mother had made to her when she'd left the funeral home.

'I thought we'd sorted your prejudice at having a female colleague.'

Hawk cleared his throat. 'My apologies,' he said unconvincingly. 'I just don't appreciate having my accuracy or efficiency questioned.'

'I'm not questioning it,' Charlotte said sincerely. 'I'm quite aware of how well you do your job, Hawk. In fact, I'd have to say I'm pretty impressed.' There. Maybe that would make him think twice about looking over her shoulder from now on. 'I just want to double-check everything. For my own peace of mind.'

'It'll be a waste of time.'

'Maybe. I'll make sure it's my time.'

'Stubborn, aren't you?' Hawk stared at her. Then he shook his head as though conceding defeat and gave one of his rare smiles. Charlotte found herself grinning instantly in response.

'Sure am. I would prefer to think of it as being tenacious, though.'

Hawk was still smiling. 'I'm sure you would.'

Charlotte found herself remembering that smile as she signed in for the collection of evidence still being held in secure storage. Funny how she could remember every occasion Hawk had smiled at her in the last few weeks. Or maybe it wasn't. The fierce lines of that uncompromising face were transformed by a smile. It was like having a glimpse of a completely different person and it was rare enough to make it memorable.

Why *didn't* Hawk smile at her very often? she wondered. She had seen him look amused and even laugh aloud when he was with his mates in the cafeteria. Was he keeping a barrier up to make sure they didn't allow friendship to creep into their working relationship? Perhaps he just didn't like her. Or maybe he was still hoping her company was only a temporary inconvenience until the wonderful Cam returned. It might complicate things if Hawk accepted how well they could work together or even, heaven forbid, started enjoying her company.

Charlotte took the cellphone back to their office. It was lunchtime and Hawk had disappeared, which was just as well. She pushed the menu buttons on the small silver phone and checked the listed calls. The last incoming call had been two hours before the crash. The final outgoing call had been late the previous evening. What had Mrs Jones meant when she'd said she blamed *him*?

'He was married, you know. He should have known better.'

The comfort being offered by relatives had made it inappropriate to ask what she meant and Charlotte had no intention of visiting Eileen Jones again now. That *would* be an intrusion and it would be getting too personally involved for her own comfort. But Katrina's mother hadn't been referring to Steve Poulsen, Charlotte was sure of that. There was someone else involved. Someone significant. She toyed with the phone, pushing the menu button again.

The whole case had grown in significance. Charlotte

wanted to clear Steve, and now that she'd stuck her neck out she *had* to. Hawk might scoff at her instinct but Charlotte had learned to trust it. If she could prove herself right, it would go a long way to proving to Hawk that she could measure up as a partner. That she could provide an element to this partnership that Cam had never supplied.

She was sick of being compared to Cam. Cam kept his files *here*. He did his scale plans on *that* paper. He kept his desk tidy enough to find things quickly and he never cluttered his work space with unnecessary items like medical textbooks or...or *hand cream!* Charlotte deliberately added to the clutter with personal items like the jar of quirky pens with fake flowers on the ends that now sat between Jamie's photo and the pump bottle of hand lotion.

Cam wouldn't have wasted his lunch-break playing with a cellphone either, but any thoughts of her absent competition faded as excitement suddenly pushed away any resentment. Charlotte pushed the buttons rapidly, reading the text messages, both received and sent. One had come in about half an hour before the accident time of 2:45 p.m.

I've told her

And the sent message was: *How did she take it?*

Not good

R U OK?

No

Want 2 meet?

Yes. Usual place?

B there in 10

The final message had been received at 2:44 p.m. *Need u babe. Where R U?*

And the final outgoing message had never been completed.

Almost th—

*   *   *

Charlotte took the paper coming out of the printer as Hawk arrived back in the office.

'Read this,' she commanded, handing over the transcript she had made of the messages. 'Text messages from Katrina Jones's cellphone.'

She had listed the times beside the lines of text. Hawk read silently. Then he looked at Charlotte, his expression one of grim comprehension.

'She was texting. That's why she didn't see the truck.'

'She probably only looked up long enough to negotiate the bend.'

'On her way to meet an upset lover who'd probably just told his wife he was leaving her.'

They looked at each other in silence for a moment. The owner of the mobile phone Katrina had been texting to would need to be interviewed. The victim impact statements already prepared for the court hearing would have to be revised. They would make compelling reading and it was almost certain that Steve Poulsen would be cleared of any blame or repercussions other than the psychological effects he was suffering. Charlotte had been right and she had picked up something that Hawk had missed or simply not thought of. She wasn't about to score points here, though. This was supposed to be a partnership, wasn't it?

'Do you want to call Steve and let him know we've found something that might put him in the clear?' she asked Hawk.

The gaze Charlotte was receiving changed. A subtle addition emerged that might have been appreciation or even an acknowledgement that a truce was being called.

'No, you do it,' Hawk said. 'You're good with people.'

Making the call that offered light at the end of a very dark tunnel for Steve Poulsen made Charlotte feel good.

But something else was making her feel even better.

'I think this might actually work out,' she told Laura that night. 'We could make a real team.'

'He obviously needs you around to make sure the job's done properly,' Laura said. 'Fancy missing something like that. I'd rub his nose in it if I were you.'

Charlotte just smiled. She didn't need to. Hawk might appear aloof and intimidating but he was aware of every nuance, however subtle, in what happened around him. He was quite capable of sensitivity. Who wouldn't be, with that degree of intelligence? He just didn't choose to show it frequently. But he had shown her…just a tiny amount and it was enough to change how she felt about her new position.

'I think I've earned some respect finally. Maybe he'll stop comparing me to Cam now.'

'If he thinks you use feminine intuition to solve a case, I have my doubts. What does he think it is? Some form of witchcraft?'

Charlotte grinned. 'Maybe it is.' Her grin faded. 'No. We're definitely making progress.'

'That's good.' Laura gave her friend a rather curious glance but Charlotte didn't feel like discussing her job or Owen Hawkins any more right now. It *was* good and Charlotte was content to simply enjoy the new space rather than try to analyse it into extinction.

Yes. Charlotte felt good.

Better than she had felt in a long, long time.

CHAPTER FOUR

THE good feeling continued. It even grew.

Steve Poulsen's lawyer was delighted with the new evidence of the text messaging.

'There's no way he'll be convicted. His driving record is exemplary. The firm that employs him was reluctant to suspend him in the first place. He's the most hard-working and reliable driver they've got.'

Jane Poulsen rang a day or two later to thank Charlotte. 'The company's taken Steve back on. He's not allowed on the road until the court case is over but they've found him work at the depot.'

'How's he feeling now?'

'He's still devastated but I think he's starting to believe in himself again. He'd got to the point where he was convinced it was all his fault. But I knew it wasn't. I kept telling him. So did Ben.'

Charlotte turned to Hawk when she'd finished the call. 'It probably wouldn't carry any weight in court but I never thought to try and take a statement from Steve's little boy.'

'He's only four. He'd say whatever he thought his dad wanted him to say.'

'But I could have asked him at the scene. He was in the passenger seat. A far better place to spot an oncoming car than a driver making a right-hand turn.'

'He might not have been looking at the road.'

'But he was. Apparently they'd been playing a game to see who could guess the colour of the next car they saw. Ben was watching for a red one.'

'Katrina's car was red.'

'Exactly! He would have won the game so he would have said something if he'd seen it. Shouted it with great excitement if he's anything like most four-year-olds I know.'

'I wouldn't know. I stay well clear of kids if at all possible.'

'Do you?' That figured. Another difference to Jamie to chalk up. Jamie had adored children and couldn't wait to have some of his own. Six, preferably.

'Yes.' The curt tone made Charlotte blink and Hawk had the grace to look slightly apologetic. 'Sorry. I shouldn't take it out on you.'

'Take what out?' The hint of apology had been mixed with something else. Charlotte didn't believe Hawk hated children. She was beginning to see through what had appeared to be impenetrable personal barriers a few weeks ago.

'My reaction to this email from Cam.' Hawk was glaring at his computer screen now. 'Seems like Cassie's got herself pregnant. There's no way he'll escape having to marry her now.'

Charlotte could feel sympathy for Hawk. He was missing his best mate after all. She couldn't help a tiny glow of something like excitement, however. This made it less likely that Cam would be returning to claim his position.

'Maybe he doesn't want to escape.'

Hawk grunted. Or maybe it was a derisive snort. Whatever it was, it signalled an end to the conversation and they both worked in silence for a while. Hawk was doing a complicated forensic map of a crime scene that had happened before Charlotte had begun working with him and she was writing up the report on a fatal bus versus pedestrian incident she had attended alone two days ago.

The interruption of Hawk speaking again was a surprise.

'I wonder what Mrs Jones is going to think when the evidence of that text messaging comes out in court.'

Charlotte was silent for a moment. The court case was coming up in a couple of weeks. The fact that Katrina had been distracted and not watching the road had been revealed but not the content of the messages.

'I think she knew about the affair her daughter was having. She made a comment at the funeral but it didn't make sense until I'd read the messages.'

'What did she say?'

'That he should have known better. That he was married. I thought at the time that it was an odd thing to say about Steve.'

'You didn't say anything to me.' Hawk sounded put out.

'No.' Charlotte couldn't suppress the tiny curl of her lips. 'I was running on feminine intuition at the time.'

Surprisingly, Hawk let the small snipe pass. He swivelled his chair so that he was facing Charlotte more directly. 'If you'd had one of those zapper things—a defibrillator—could you have saved Mr Jones?'

'We call them "toasters" in the trade.' Charlotte smiled but then became serious. 'It's impossible to know, Hawk. We would have known exactly what we were dealing with if we could have seen the rhythm, though. If it *had* been a VF arrest and we'd shocked him early, it might have made a difference. Earlier drug therapy might have helped too but you can't just administer cardiac drugs blindly.'

'So why don't you carry a "toaster"?'

'You've seen how big a life pack that has a display screen is. You made enough fuss about finding room for my kit in the car.'

Hawk didn't even seem to notice this second snipe. 'You can't know how useful something is until you're in a situation where you need it and it's not available.'

'It's hardly likely to be something we'd need on a regular

basis. A cardiac arrest following trauma is very unlikely to be treatable. We drive a squad car, not an ambulance.' Charlotte shook her head. 'And I hope we're never going to have people that weren't even involved in a crash falling over on us again.'

'How many lives would you have to save to make it worthwhile carrying one?' Hawk didn't seem to want to let the matter drop.

'Depends on the value you put on a life, I guess.' Charlotte was not being facetious. 'They cost tens of thousands of dollars, Hawk. Police administration would not see it as a cost-effective budget item even it you could prove it might save ten lives. A hundred even.' Besides, she felt like adding, you're not planning to work with me on anything more than a temporary basis. What would you and Cam do with a life pack after he comes back?

'You're probably right.' The end to the conversation was abrupt as Hawk turned back to his computer, but Charlotte found it more difficult to concentrate on her report now. She was detailing circumstances, which included the fact that the bus driver's shift had been due to finish in fifteen minutes and that he had been more than ordinarily tired because he'd been out with the boys the night before to watch a rugby match at the pub. Reaching for a notepad, Charlotte scribbled a note she would use when adding her conclusions and opinions to the end of the report. It seemed fairly obvious that the driver's reaction times were bound to have been slower than normal and even if he hadn't been travelling a little over the speed limit he might still have been unable to stop when someone had simply stepped out onto a pedestrian crossing. It didn't excuse the driver, however, and Charlotte would be recommending that several charges be laid.

She stole a glance over her shoulder as she finished the rapid notes and caught Hawk's profile. He looked intent on his task but clearly he had found the mental energy to consider something irrelevant. How often did he think about Stan Jones? The case had been significant in more ways than one. Charlotte might need to revise her opinion that her professional relationship with Owen Hawkins had undergone a sea change when she'd earned respect by hunting down the new evidence in this case.

Maybe the change had really occurred earlier, unnoticed due to the dramatic nature of the influence. The first measurable respect she had earned from Hawk had come during that resuscitation on Stan Jones, when she had been using every skill of her 'other' career—the skills Hawk had resented her bringing to her job as a crash investigator.

Hawk had been out of his depth then. Frightened, even. Charlotte had seen that flash of vulnerability and while it had made no difference at the time she had remembered it vividly later. She had welcomed the sense of power it had bestowed on her and it had, without doubt, heralded a change in the way they worked together. But had her softening towards Hawk come from embracing a feeling of superiority or had it been more that his vulnerability had made him seem more human somehow? Charlotte had depended on his assistance at the time and she had sympathised with his fear. Nobody could remain unaffected when another person was dying in front of them. He had risen to the challenge, too. Admirably, in fact.

Yes. Charlotte turned back to her report with confidence that she could concentrate, having identified the elusive emotion that had been nagging somewhere in the back of her mind. The growing respect in the atmosphere wasn't just one-sided. Owen Hawkins had attributes that went beyond his abilities as a crash investigator. Charlotte resolved to stop trying to find fault with Hawk. To stop comparing him to Jamie all the time and to stop—or at least *try* to stop—the conversational sniping they had both indulged in ever since she'd started this job.

An already positive mood consolidated into something like inspiration. Charlotte would cease working independently, alongside rather than with Hawk. She had already proved she was capable of competing with the perfect ex-partner, hadn't she? Maybe it was time to see what they could do as a team.

Hawk noticed the difference on the next job they attended. It wasn't a fatal crash but one of those involved was badly injured so it could become one. That meant that all relevant information still had to be gathered, which was a pain because the scene was a complicated one. Five roads entered this intersection and one of those roads was a favourite haunt for young people to test out their modified hot-rods on Friday nights. Both he and Charlotte were wandering around holding cans of spray paint.

'There's tyre marks for Africa, isn't there?' Charlotte groaned. 'And I've found what look like gouge marks from more than one rollover.'

'Boy racers,' Hawk informed her.

Charlotte grinned. 'So that sixty-year-old woman who's in Intensive Care now was out for a Friday night with a difference?'

'She was in the wrong place at the wrong time.' Hawk shook his can of paint and the ball rattled like a drum roll. 'This is her braking mark.'

Hawk's tone was only mildly challenging. He fully expected to have his opinions questioned now and Charlotte had a wealth of ammunition she could muster. The marks he had chosen were criss-crossed with other marks, the ages of which were all debatable. He was looking forward to countering the arguments with his observations on tyre width, tread pattern and tyre inflation levels.

'I think you're right,' Charlotte said instead. 'I'll mark the debris pattern before all this glass gets swept up, shall I?'

Hawk found himself re-examining the other tyre marks to provide the arguments he had been sure would be forthcoming from his partner. Still confident his conclusion was correct, he sprayed paint lines to isolate the marks but the whole business felt mechanical somehow. Unsatisfying.

A brisk mental shake was in order here. He and Cam had never indulged in heated debates on scene about the relevance of evidence. He should be appreciating the fact that Charlotte had finally decided his opinion was justified and there was no point in challenging him. Instead, Hawk found himself watching Charlotte as she set up the theodolite and his dissatisfaction grew. The sparring over the last month had been a pain. Charlotte had a tendency to remember everything he said and didn't hesitate to throw it back at him. He was still getting jibes about her prerogative to change her mind or references to 'fluffing around' on scene. And she seemed to take pleasure in challenging everything.

Even basics like weather and light conditions. Only last week she had been delighted to pounce on a sentence in a report he'd completed.

'It *was* overcast,' Hawk had responded defensively. 'The light was poor due to the heavy cloud cover.'

'That was an hour after the crash.'

'It had been cloudy for hours. It started to rain while we were there. Heavily. Have you forgotten the problem we had with evidence getting washed away? Or that I went and found you a coat?'

'Of course not.' A quick smile had lifted the corners of Charlotte's mouth. 'I appreciated the coat. But you know how fast a southerly front can sweep in. Cloud cover prior to that was patchy. If there *had* been a break in the clouds

at that time of day, then the angle of sun would have been
in a line that could have caused enough glare to blind the
driver to the colour of the traffic lights. See? I've drawn
the angle in...here.'

'Other cars managed to stop.'

'Maybe they had their visors in the right position. Or
they were wearing sunglasses.'

'It's not going to make any difference to the outcome of
this investigation.'

'It's a factor that shouldn't be ignored.'

'If we spent our time investigating every remote possibility, we'd never cope with our workload. What are you
suggesting? That we chase down witnesses and visit the
meteorological office to find out whether there *might* have
been a break in cloud cover at that particular time?'

'No. I just think we should consider anything that might
be relevant and that details in a written report should be as
accurate as possible.'

'Fine,' Hawk had growled. 'Give it back and I'll change
the wording in the damn report.'

Witness interviews provided ample grounds for differences of opinion as well. Charlotte had an uncanny ability
to detect whether someone was telling the truth.

'Of course he was lying. Didn't you notice how often he
licked his lips? And the way you could see his heart rate
increase by his carotid pulse?'

Hawk hadn't noticed. The statement had been delivered
calmly and had been plausible enough to fit the evidence.
The uncomfortable question of just how well he'd been
doing his job before Charlotte had come along wasn't worth
worrying about. Nobody had ever made a complaint. But
would he have discovered those text messages and changed
someone's life from a picture of devastation as Charlotte
had done for Steve Poulsen? Possibly not. And while Hawk
was confident enough that his analysis of today's scene was

accurate, he *wanted* to get tested, dammit. It was much more satisfying to be sure of something by arguing away any other possibilities.

And…and he *enjoyed* arguing with Charlotte. It provided a spark that his camaraderie with Cam had never had. He'd always been wary of smart women. They were too capable of analysing everything and either deciphering an incorrect message and getting upset or staying too many steps ahead, which provided a huge advantage in any plan for manipulation. But that was on a personal level. Hawk had never *worked* closely with a woman before and Charlotte's intelligence and capability for lateral thinking complemented his own thought processes perfectly. He could harness it—especially via a heated exchange in which they were both out to prove themselves right—and between them they would make an unbeatable team.

Hawk shrugged off the notion. There was no point in getting excited at such a possibility when this was a temporary situation. And it was stupid to have the urge to provoke an argument to add some spice to his job. Better that Charlotte kept up this agreeable mood and became less interesting to have around. He suppressed a smile as he dropped the can of spray paint back into its crate. She wouldn't be able to keep it up for long anyway.

She was way too feisty for that.

His colleagues thought it was all very amusing.

'So…what's the stroppy one been up to this week?'

'Not much,' Hawk was forced to admit. Mind you, even if Charlotte *had* provided some annoying interlude he suddenly didn't feel the least bit inclined to offer it up as lunchtime entertainment for his cronies. He could sense their disappointment as he unwrapped his filled roll. Had his complaints about his new partner become that much of their routine? 'We've been flat out,' he said casually. 'Too busy to do anything other than co-operate with total professional harmony.'

'Ha!' Murphy's snort said it all. 'That'll be the day.'

'So, have you changed your mind about working with a chick, then, Hawk?'

'This particular chick might be an exception,' Hawk conceded.

'Uh-oh! She's got under his skin at last.'

Hawk's snort was intended to be dismissive and not simply for the benefit of his companions. 'She's damned good at her job.'

'Which one?'

A wry smile acknowledged Hawk's past complaints about working with a crash investigator who was also a paramedic. They seemed a long time ago now. 'Both, actually,' he said. 'It's quite helpful occasionally. We wanted information on the condition of someone in ICU yesterday, to gauge whether the job was going to turn into a fatal. I hit a brick wall but Charlie went to some doctor she knows in Emergency and he got all the info we needed in five minutes flat.'

His mates didn't seem particularly interested in discussing Charlotte Laing's virtues. Murphy's eyes were just about on stalks.

'Check *that* out.'

'What?' Young Brent Jackson followed the direction of Murphy's gaze and whistled softly in appreciation. 'Whoa! She must be the new girl in the control room.'

Hawk's gaze flicked automatically to the queue at the cafeteria counter. The object of virtually every male in the room's attention was instantly obvious. Very young, very blonde and very, very pretty. Her uniform did little to detract from her curves and the slightly shy, wide-eyed observation of her unfamiliar environment was appealing.

There would be no shortage of new colleagues to help her find her way around, that was for sure.

'Just your type, Hawk.'

He shrugged. The newcomer *was* just his type. A month ago his heart rate might well have jumped with the potential of a new pursuit and satisfying victory. Right now, he was more interested in eating his lunch. Continued appreciative remarks from his colleagues became almost irritating. They were all adult men, weren't they, not testosterone-laden teenagers? What was so instantly attractive about blondes, anyway? Charlotte had been right. You had to be pretty shallow to get fixated on a hair colour that probably came out of a bottle anyway.

Hawk picked up his apple and abandoned his coffee. 'Better head back to the office. Catch you guys later.'

Irritation had definitely set in by the time he reached his desk. Hair colour was meaningless. Same went for breast size. Murphy had been virtually drooling when he'd caught a closer view of the blonde's attributes in that department as she'd passed their table. Why the hell wasn't Cam around? He needed a thrashing on the squash court. Or a session at the rifle range.

'That's what I need,' Hawk said aloud. The physical jolt of firing a high-powered weapon and the satisfaction of hitting a target was exactly what might do the trick. It took him a minute or two to locate the telephone directory so he could arrange a visit. Annoyingly, but not surprisingly, it turned up in the mess on Charlotte's desk. Or maybe it wasn't so annoying. He tucked the complaint away as future ammunition. How could she hope to do her job efficiently when she couldn't keep her work space tidy? The only clear part of her desk was the corner with the silly bunch of fake flower pens and that photograph of her dead fiancé.

Hawk eyed the photograph with distaste. The guy was

good-looking enough and certainly had the kind of smile that added credence to the legend of his popularity but, from what Hawk had heard, he hadn't been the saint Charlotte made him out to be. Hawk had asked someone. More than one person, actually. Turned out that Jamie Forrest had been drinking the night of his fatal crash. Not over the limit as it had been then but enough to impair anyone's judgement. And he'd been in the car with four of his mates. Some kind of extra stag do in the run-up to his wedding. What the hell had he been doing out with mates, anyway? If Hawk was engaged to Charlotte he would have been spending his time with *her*.

The telephone directory hit his desk with a resounding slap. Where the hell had *that* come from?

Him…engaged?

To Charlotte Laing?

The very notion was as disturbing as that acute awareness of her had been the first morning they'd met. When he'd seen her with that patient and had noticed her hands and experienced that bizarre curiosity about what it would feel like to have her touch *him*. He'd got through that. Dismissed it.

Hadn't he?

The telephone remained untouched and Hawk stared at a page in the listings that was half a book away from the rifle range. A flood of suppressed images played through his mind.

Charlotte crouched at a roadside, looking up with excitement because she'd found some unexpected piece of evidence.

The way she smiled…slowly…which made her amusement or just a greeting that much more significant.

The way she flicked that long rope of hair back over her shoulder, which Hawk had come to learn was a signal that he was in for some kind of confrontation.

The way those golden-brown eyes could light and change with determination, laughter, thoughtfulness or anger.

He could only imagine what they would be like, burning with a physical passion. Not that he was about to touch her, of course.

No way!

She'd made her views of 'being hit on' abundantly clear the first day she'd been here. In this very office. And even if they weren't working together, what chance would he have had? Zilch. That blasted photograph on her desk advertised that like a neon sign. She was still in love with a ghost and she had no intention of letting any flesh and blood compete.

What a waste.

What a damned, stupid waste!

CHAPTER FIVE

IT WAS only a matter of time before Charlotte and Hawk had to spend a night together.

The area covered by the investigative unit was wide and a high-speed crash on a country road was more likely to produce a fatal result than an incident within city limits. Deploying resources to an isolated area more than once was undesirable so the Serious Crash Squad was required to stay as long as it took to collect the evidence they needed from the scene.

Charlotte rang Laura on receiving news of the callout. 'I won't be home tonight,' she told her flatmate. 'We've got a multiple fatality incident out in the sticks. We're only going to have an hour or so of daylight by the time we get there so we'll have to finish the job in the morning.'

'Oh, no! Not tonight of all nights!'

'It's probably a good thing.' Charlotte tried to sound positive. 'I wouldn't have been very good company.'

'But I was going to drag you out to a movie or something and take your mind off things. I've got a bottle of wine in the fridge, too. I thought with you not being on call you could get wasted if you felt like it.'

'We'll get the job done much quicker if we both go.'

'Where are you going to sleep? In the car?'

'No. It's only about twenty kilometres out of Masterton so they've organised a motel for us.'

'Good grief. A whole night with Hawk. That's all you need right now.'

'I'm sure they've given us separate rooms.' It was supposed to be a joke but why did it give Charlotte a weird

84

sensation in the pit of her stomach to have even allowed the hint of an alternative option to enter her mind? Admitting, even to herself, that Hawk was an attractive man smacked of disloyalty to Jamie. To allow any notion of sharing a room with him to surface was unthinkable. Especially today.

'I'd sleep in the car otherwise, if I were you.' At least Laura had found the notion amusing. Her laughter faded quickly, however. 'Do you need me to drop anything in for you? I'm still at home.'

'No. Thanks anyway but I'm walking into the car park right now. I keep an overnight bag in the car. These sorts of trips happen quite frequently in this game. I'm surprised we haven't had one before this.'

'Well, I'm just sorry it's happened today. Will you be OK?'

'Sure.' Charlotte injected a firm note into her tone. 'It's been two years. It's got to be easier this time.'

The subdued atmosphere in the squad car was unmistakable.

'Nice afternoon for a trip to the country.'

'Yes, it is.'

'It's one of the things I love about this job. You never know what's just around the corner. Where you're going to be.'

'No.'

'Got your toothbrush?'

'Yes.'

Hawk gave up trying to make conversation. He could guess why Charlotte seemed so withdrawn. She hated the idea of spending a night out of town in his company. He fiddled with the radio until he tuned into a 'classic hits' station and something cheerful from Abba filled the silence in the car. He hadn't been so keen on this development himself. It had had to come, of course. In fact, it was surprising they'd managed to work together for well over a month without it happening, but Hawk couldn't afford to think of the possibilities it presented.

And he was completely unable to prevent himself doing so.

It was a relief to end the ninety-minute car trip and to get stuck into the job at hand. Three people had been killed and two seriously injured from the two vehicles involved so it was a major incident. A family of four had been in the late-model sedan. The driver of the sheep truck had been alone. The wrecks had not been found until a farm worker, who had heard the impact, had taken his trail bike across four paddocks to investigate and the survivors had been unable to give any clues to what had happened.

The bodies of the victims, including a child, had been removed by the time Hawk and Charlotte arrived, but the wrecks were still largely untouched and the road had been closed by the local police officer to protect the scene.

'It's no problem,' he assured the squad members. 'This road isn't used that much anyway and it's easy enough to reroute traffic. The ford on the next road doesn't close at this time of year. You guys take all the time you need.' He shook his head as he took another long glance around them. 'Bit of a mess, isn't it?'

'Sure is,' Hawk agreed. 'We'll need a crane to get that sheep truck upright. Just as well it was empty.'

'Yeah. A couple of hundred dead and injured sheep to work around wouldn't be much fun.'

It wasn't much fun anyway. Hawk might be getting used to Charlotte being less argumentative on scene but he'd never seen her in the kind of mood she was in today. He couldn't put his finger on what was different and it bothered him. Not that she was doing anything wrong.

'This looks like it could be the first contact point. It's just prior to that puddle of radiator fluid.'

Hawk wasn't going to query the nature of the liquid still visible on the surface of the road. The green shine of anti-freeze was obvious.

'And there's the start of the crooks in the skid mark.'

Hawk took photographs of the sharp bends in the skid marks. Skids were generally straight and even throughout their length because a vehicle tended to slide in a straight line unless deflected by some external force. A swerve was a deviation caused by reasons other than impact with some object. A crook often indicated the end of the pre-collision skid marks and the start of the post-collision marks. They could occur at the same time in more than one skid mark and front crooks could move in one direction while the rear crooks moved in the opposite direction.

In this case it became more complicated because there was a second set of crook marks in what appeared to be a yaw. The tyre marks from the car ended abruptly at that point.

'Two impact points?' Charlotte queried. It was unlike her to request an opinion rather than offer one, but Hawk was too focussed to take much notice. Multiple impact points were less likely in a crash involving only two vehicles. Or maybe not in this case.

'We've got an unloaded semi-trailer on the other vehicle,' he said aloud. 'The braking marks show axle twist which had lifted the trailer body. If the front wheels had locked, the steering ability would have been lost and it could have jackknifed. Maybe the trailer hit the car again with enough force to get it airborne.'

'But front axle brakes are designed to prevent jackknifing.' The challenge was half-hearted, however. 'It's an old truck. I'll check its certification and see when it last had a warrant of fitness.'

The light was fading before they had done more than what seemed a cursory inspection of the scene and recorded as much as they could. Charlotte used a torch as she walked around the wrecks.

'Might have something here, Hawk.'

'What's that?' Hawk was still shaking his head at the total devastation of the sedan involved in the crash. It was a miracle there had been survivors. The occupant of the truck might have come through alive if he hadn't been ejected from the cab as the heavy vehicle had tipped onto its side, but truck drivers weren't known to take the trouble to wear safety belts.

'He was driving illegally. The road tax certificate is twenty thousand kilometres overdue.' While diesel was a cheaper fuel to use for commercial vehicles, the equivalent of petrol tax was taken when drivers had to purchase kilometres of road use in advance.

'Maybe he was slack about mechanical fitness as well.'

'I forgot to check when I was looking at the odometer.' Charlotte shone her torch towards the stickers on the inside of the windscreen above her. 'And I can't see from here. I'll climb up again, shall I?'

'It's getting too dark to be safe clambering around here. Let's call it a day and find that motel, shall we?' Hawk was more than ready to call an end to the long day. 'We can do all this in the morning and I don't know about you, but I'm starving.'

Charlotte's breath escaped in a sigh as she nodded. 'Sure.'

Was it the thought of leaving a job half-finished that was disappointing or was the problem more likely to be the prospect of sharing an evening meal with him in the pub of the small town they were heading for? Well, they didn't *have* to eat together if she felt like that. Hawk flicked an offended glance in Charlotte's direction but she was shining her torch again on that road tax certificate on the lower edge of the truck beside a front tyre. Hawk could feel his expression changing.

That was it. Finding that type of clue usually made Charlotte light up like a Christmas tree, but there was not even a hint of sparkle there right now. It confirmed his general impression that she was running on automatic. Charlotte's mind had not really been on the job today.

Something wasn't right.

'It's none of my business,' Hawk told himself firmly as he had a quick wash in his motel unit a little later.

So why did it bother him so much?

Surprisingly, Charlotte hadn't shown any sign of reluctance when he'd suggested they meet for dinner. Having been pleased at the time, Hawk changed his mind when he saw her emerge from the neighbouring motel unit. Hell, *he* should have been the one to suggest they make their own arrangements for the evening. He'd never seen her out of uniform before. The faded denim jeans and a soft woollen top wasn't exactly getting dressed up but it made her seem far more approachable on a personal level somehow. It was the hair that really gave him a kick in the guts, however. He'd never seen it out of that tightly twisted rope. Now it was loose, hanging in a shining, dark curtain that covered her back to her waist, and it had a sort of ripple in it that the plaiting had probably encouraged. And suddenly Hawk knew that he would never be even remotely attracted to blond tresses again.

It was just as well he was so hungry. Concentrating on dealing with the generous serving of steak and chips he ordered at the pub kept his mind at least partly centred on physical needs he could do something about. The conversation helped, too, as Charlotte seemed determined to keep their communication on a business level and discuss nothing that didn't relate to the case they were on. It wasn't until the edges of Hawk's hunger had been well and truly blunted that he noticed Charlotte's plate. Her meal of fish and chips was virtually untouched.

'You're not eating much, Charlie. Nothing wrong with the food, is there?'

'No. It's great. I'm just not very hungry.'

'Are you sick?'

'No.'

Hawk ate in silence for another minute. It *was* his business if something affected his partner, wasn't it? If Charlotte was going to be moody and difficult to work with, then he had the right to know why, surely? He might even be able to help.

'You've been kind of quiet all day.'

'I thought you liked me being quiet. No mind-changing. No fluffing.'

Hawk smiled even though the reference to what had become a joke between them was as half-hearted as most of Charlotte's comments that day. She was certainly trying to supply a normal response and encourage him to mind his own business but Hawk had had enough.

'What's wrong?' he asked bluntly.

'Nothing.'

'Is it this job?' Hawk ignored the fact that she had been quiet well before the call had come in. 'It's pretty rough when kids are involved. Those five-year-olds were twins.'

'The victims were long gone by the time we got here. I'm probably more used to dealing with that kind of thing than you are, anyway.'

'So you're not upset?'

'Of course not.'

But to his horror Hawk saw that he had prised the lid off something she was clearly trying to keep buried. The shine of sudden tears was only glimpsed momentarily but he could see how hard she was blinking now as she stared determinedly at the food still cooling on the plate in front of her. He frowned as his remaining appetite deserted him. He pushed his plate to one side and leaned forward just enough to indicate his willingness to listen.

'Do you want to tell me about it?'

He must have managed to convey a genuine personal interest. Charlotte's eyes widened in surprise and then filled again with tears. This time she didn't manage to control them. One spilled out to roll down the side of her nose and Hawk had to resist the strong impulse to reach out and brush it away. He watched in fascination as it trickled into the corner of her mouth and the tip of Charlotte's tongue appeared to collect it. The realisation that this woman wasn't as tough as she made out was a bit of an eye-opener. This was a part of her that Hawk hadn't been allowed to see. A vulnerable part. Something twisted deep within Hawk. He wasn't sure what it was but its unfamiliarity made it distinctly uncomfortable.

'It's…it's today,' Charlotte finally admitted with obvious reluctance.

'What about today? This job?' Hawk tried to step back from his desire to get involved. He didn't want a repeat of that odd sensation in his gut so he made his tone deliberately light. 'Hey, it's not because I was moaning about how long it took you to get ready, is it? You still found what you needed, which was a minor miracle considering the mess your desk was in.'

Charlotte tried to look offended but failed miserably. She shook her head in the silence that followed and then took a deep breath as though a decision had been made. 'I meant the date,' she said slowly. 'It's a kind of anniversary.'

'Oh.' Hawk sat back in his chair again, his heart sinking. He might have guessed. He didn't want to talk about it but now he had no choice, did he? 'Something to do with Jamie, is it?'

She nodded. 'It would have been our wedding anniversary today…if we'd got married.'

Hawk said nothing. He watched Charlotte struggle not to let any further tears escape. She blew her nose. She fiddled with her knife and fork.

'Sorry,' she said eventually. 'I was determined not to let this happen. It's ridiculous after all this time.'

Hawk fought the impulse to agree. It had been years ago. Charlotte needed to stop mourning and start living again. Really living. This was personal ground that he hadn't felt any inclination to step on. His reaction to having the reminder of Jamie Forrest in their office on a permanent basis was such that he knew Charlotte would be very unlikely to want to discuss the subject with him but, for heaven's sake, it was no wonder it annoyed him.

Charlotte had way too much going for her to turn herself into a nun. For such an intelligent woman she was making a huge mistake. If he was a friend, he would offer comfort. Allow her to wallow in her sadness and get it out of her system, at least temporarily. But he wasn't a friend and, anyway, it was the last thing Charlotte needed. What she really needed was someone who could try and make her see sense and move on. And maybe he was just the person to do it.

What did he have to lose after all? They were nearly halfway through their period of being colleagues. So what if the atmosphere got a little frosty? He wouldn't have to put up with it for long and it would be worth it if it did something to help Charlotte.

The impression of genuine warmth had been Charlotte's undoing. The way Hawk had leaned across the table towards her. The expression of personal concern in his eyes. Not to mention the astonishing thought that he might be about to reach across the table and take hold of her hand or something.

Whatever it was, it had opened the door that had always been a little ajar on this date. Even now, when Hawk had leaned back in his chair and increased the distance between them, she didn't feel like strengthening the crumbling barriers she'd kept around this particular subject. She *needed* to talk to someone and Hawk had the only available set of ears. She would leave it up to him, however. If he really didn't want that kind of personal communication, she would have to deal with it alone. Charlotte rearranged her cutlery yet again. It was up to Hawk. If the next words he spoke were changing the subject then, as far as she was concerned, the subject would never be raised between them again.

'How long had you known Jamie?'

The unexpected relief at the invitation to continue talking about him prompted a wistful smile. 'Only three months.'

'And you were about to get married?'

'Jamie was killed the night before the wedding.'

Hawk's head was shaking as though he found it unbelievable, but the look Charlotte was receiving suggested astonishment rather than sympathy. 'It's beyond me,' he muttered cryptically.

'What is?'

'Well, for a start, I'm kind of curious why Jamie would have been out on the town with his mates instead of spending time with you.'

'How did you know he was out with his mates?'

'I've heard things. People talk.'

'He had a lot of friends,' Charlotte said defensively. 'Some of them had been working on the night of his stag do. He got persuaded to spend some time with them. *I* didn't mind.' Charlotte stared at Hawk. 'So why the hell should it bother *you*?'

'I have no idea,' Hawk admitted. 'Mind you, it's also beyond me the way some people rush into marriage like that. It's no wonder most marriages fail.'

Charlotte could feel her face tightening. She was accustomed to acknowledgement of her personal tragedy. To have someone take the view that the marriage would never have lasted anyway was an unexpected and downright nasty reaction. How could she have thought she'd detected kindness and compassion in the way Hawk had broached this subject?

'Are you suggesting that my marriage to Jamie would have failed?'

'Not necessarily.' Hawk seemed to be relishing the fact that he was making her angry instead of giving her a chance to share her grief. How could she have been starting to think she might even *like* him? The man was a complete bastard.

'Cam's done the same thing,' Hawk said. 'He started talking marriage within days of meeting Cassie. Claimed it was love at first sight.'

'It *can* happen,' Charlotte said coldly.

Hawk's snort was dismissive. 'Only on a physical level. Because that's all you can know about in that space of time. It's attraction. Lust. The stirring of hormones. I've been there myself, believe it or not. I *do* know what I'm talking about.'

His glance away from Charlotte was clearly deliberate and she felt a flash of satisfaction. Good. Her appalled glare was having the effect of making him feel uncomfortable.

'Sure, it's powerful.' Hawk's voice had an oddly strangled note to it and he cleared his throat before continuing. 'And I can understand why some people get carried away, but any intelligent person knows it's not going to last. It's not love.'

'And you're an expert?' Charlotte asked scathingly. 'How old are you, Hawk? Thirty-five?'

'Thirty-six.'

'The age that most men have chosen a partner for life, then.'

'No—the age that most people are starting to realise they've made a mistake. The attraction has worn off and they're trapped by responsibilities they can't escape.'

It was Charlotte's turn to snort incredulously. Hawk had the kind of battle light in his eyes that arguing about the relevance of road evidence usually engendered, but Charlotte had no intention of letting him win this argument. 'You're so incredibly cynical, Owen Hawkins. Of course the initial attraction changes. That's when it gets replaced by something deeper. Respect…and friendship…and *commitment*. The kind of stuff you wouldn't know anything about because you probably never hang around long enough to find out.'

'You can't know that's going to happen. Not until you've been with someone long enough. A few weeks, months even—what kind of basis is that to commit yourself for the rest of your life?'

'You've obviously never been in love.'

'Actually, I have.'

Charlotte was taken aback. Who was she? And how had she felt when Hawk had dumped her? 'But you've never been married.'

'I was engaged. It's a long time ago now.'

Charlotte gave her head a tiny shake. Just enough to flick some stray locks of hair away from her face. 'And how long did you wait to decide to get engaged?'

'Two years.' The gaze holding her own was steady. 'I don't commit myself to anything that I'm not absolutely sure I can deliver.'

'So what happened to the delivery?' Charlotte wasn't

about to offer any sympathy on some romance that hadn't worked out for Hawk. He didn't deserve any. The way he had verbally bullied her away from receiving any comfort over Jamie had been remarkably hurtful. She kept her tone uncharacteristically waspish. 'Did you choose the wrong address?'

'In a manner of speaking. She changed her mind. She "fell in love" with my best mate at the time.'

'Oh.' So Hawk had been the one to get dumped. It still didn't mean he deserved any sympathy, though. Did it?

'They got married,' Hawk continued evenly. 'Had a couple of kids and then got divorced three years later.'

'Oh.' It was hardly an intelligent response but Charlotte had caught something she doubted that Hawk wanted her to read from his expression. He *had* been hurt badly. Heartbroken, maybe. Her tone softened a little. 'That must have been rough.'

Hawk shrugged. 'It was an experience I have no wish to repeat.'

Charlotte smiled. 'What is it they say? Experience is something you get when you don't get what you want.'

'Valuable lessons in life. At least you can use them to define what you really want. Or, in my case, what you *don't* want.'

'Like marriage?'

'Precisely. Life's too short. And if you narrow your options too far, you're going to miss out.'

'Maybe you miss out if you *don't* narrow your options.'

'Meaning?'

'Marriage is the only kind of arrangement I'd want to have kids in. Have you never wanted to have a child? Do you really hate them that much?'

Hawk shrugged. 'I got over that a long time ago.'

'At the same time you got over your broken engagement?'

Hawk's pupils widened but he looked away before Charlotte could try and analyse his reaction. 'What about you?' he asked.

'Yeah,' Charlotte said softly. 'I wanted kids.'

'And *how* old are you, Charlie?'

'Thirty-two.'

'It's not too late, then.'

'But it is.' Charlotte shut her eyes for a moment. 'It became too late the moment Jamie died.'

Speaking his name was almost a surprise and Charlotte realised that she hadn't even been thinking of him for several minutes now. Ever since Hawk had launched this debate about marriage, in fact. Amazing, considering how difficult it had been for her to think of anything else today.

The reminder of what had led up to this solitary meal with her partner gave Charlotte an excuse to try and change the subject. She and Hawk were colleagues. They shared the same career. A career that she had chosen to be the focus of her life from now on. She gave a small but decisive shake of her head.

'So you needn't worry about my biological clock interfering with my career. Any more than yours will.'

'You got over wanting kids?' Hawk's tone was sceptical.

'It's not going to happen.'

'Why, because Jamie isn't going to be their father?'

Damn the man. Why couldn't he drop the subject? He'd succeeded in distracting her, which might be disloyal but not entirely unwelcome. What was he trying to do now? Make sure she got upset all over again?

'Precisely.' Her glance was intended to hurt Hawk as much as his comment had wounded her. 'I've never met a man who can hold a candle to Jamie Forrest and I don't expect to. I'm not about to settle for second best.'

'What a waste,' Hawk murmured.

Charlotte blinked. 'I'm flattered that you would consider me such a good prospective mother.'

'It wasn't parenthood I was considering.'

And suddenly Hawk's gaze held something Charlotte had anticipated even less than his odd reaction to her earlier distress. It was the kind of appreciation that she saw in the eyes of many men she met. Was it just because it was so unexpected that her normal reaction was difficult to summon? She should be furious that Hawk had chosen such an inappropriate moment to reveal the fact that he fancied her. Her body was mounting some kind of rebellion, however, and Charlotte couldn't quell the host of butterflies suddenly let loose in her stomach.

She looked down at her plate of food. Her stomach was empty, that was probably what was causing the sensation. She picked up a cold chip. 'I'm not interested in casual sex,' she informed Hawk. 'And I don't expect—or even want—to meet anyone that would interest me longer term. Bit of a Catch-22 situation really.'

'You mean there hasn't been anyone…since Jamie?'

'That is a very personal question.' Charlotte dropped the chip. She still had no desire to eat.

'We're partners. A good partnership means a level of friendship. Trust. Respect. The kind of relationship Cam and I had.' Hawk smiled. 'Like a good marriage, really. Without the sex, of course.'

'Of course.' The more blatant reference to sex made talking about it less of a shock, but it still gave those butterflies another burst of energy. Talking about sex with Hawk was not a good idea. It highlighted the fact that they were a man and a woman. Hawk had, however inadvertently, revealed the fact that he was attracted to her. Charlotte could only hope like hell he hadn't received a similar message from her. She might have been very aware of Hawk right from when they had first met but she *wasn't* attracted to him. Butterflies could lie. Couldn't they?

This was a dangerous space. But maybe Hawk was offering something else. A partnership that matched what he'd had with Cam. Real acceptance. Could she afford to turn that down? Maybe she could kill two birds with one stone here, accept a possible overture to a friendship and deny any attraction at the same time.

'OK, partner,' she said as lightly as she could manage. 'No. There's been no one since Jamie. I haven't been remotely interested.'

'Really? You haven't even met anyone who's *remotely* attractive?'

Was he fishing? Charlotte could feel her heart thumping with uncomfortable speed. She should simply say no and cut off any possibility of seeing that look in Hawk's eyes again. It should have been an easy thing to say but somehow Charlotte's lips were refusing to co-operate.

'I wouldn't say that…exactly.'

He knew. That satisfied gleam in the depths of those dark blue eyes were a dead give-away. He knew something that Charlotte was only just beginning to realise herself. An attraction existed between them.

A mutual attraction.

What the hell was she going to say if he suggested doing something about it? And would her body and lips co-operate with the orders she knew her brain and, more importantly, her heart would issue? Especially today. Appallingly, it took a second or two for Charlotte to remember just why it would be so inappropriate today.

'I've never worked closely with a woman before.' Hawk's tone was casual. Was he trying to move off dangerous ground himself?

'Perhaps it'll be a valuable life lesson,' Charlotte quipped. The sooner they reached verbal safety, the better.

She smiled at Hawk, confident that she could extricate herself now.

But Hawk's grin was completely disarming. 'I have hopes that it might be a very positive experience. Mind you, I have to confess I didn't think so to start with.'

'No kidding.' Charlotte's smile felt real for the first time that day. 'I would never have guessed.'

'You weren't what I expected.' Hawk cleared his throat. 'So far, I'm very impressed. You're a lot more competent than I thought you would be—both as a paramedic and a crash investigator.'

'Thanks…I think.'

'You're also a lot more attractive than I expected.'

Charlotte couldn't look at him. No way. Heaven only knew what it might give away. 'Is that a problem?'

'I thought I had it taped but it seems like the jury just absconded again before the final verdict was in. I don't like distractions.'

'It's up to you not to be distracted, then, isn't it?'

'Precisely. And that's something I can cope with unless…'

Hawk must like being precise, Charlotte thought vaguely. She was trying to decide what had stirred up the butterflies again. There was something different about Hawk's voice. Always deep, it seemed almost liquid right now. It was rippling over Charlotte and oozing into places that set nerve endings alight. This was crazy. She was *not* attracted to Owen Hawkins. Not like that, anyway. Charlotte almost gulped.

'Unless what?'

'Unless the distraction is mutual.'

Charlotte had to fight the urge to close her eyes and bask in the heat his voice was generating. *How* could this have happened? And what would happen if she admitted the attraction was mutual? If he touched her…or even just continued speaking to her like that, the temptation to explore this desire that had ambushed her might be irresistible. It was unthinkable. Purely physical, of course, but still unthinkable.

'I'm here to do a job, Hawk. I'm not about to let anything...or anyone...interfere with that.'

The quirk of a single eyebrow was irritating. She had seen it before when Hawk had some piece of information available that he knew would allow him victory in whatever it was they were debating. This wasn't a professional matter, however. Or was it?

'I read my contract,' Charlotte added hastily. 'The clause about not letting personal relationships between colleagues interfere with the functioning of a department was rather clear, I thought.'

'It's probably not something that Elsie would approve of, I have to admit.'

'The way I read it, it can result in the immediate transfer of an officer to another department or even station. We don't work in a highly populated branch of the police force, Hawk. Opportunities for transfer would be rather limited.' And she would be the one to get the chop. Last on, first off.

'Almost non-existent,' Hawk agreed.

'I've worked far too hard to get where I am. I'm not about to lose my job.'

'Neither am I.'

'I'm glad we understand each other.'

'Oh, so am I.'

But Hawk's smile was suspiciously pleased. Had Charlotte succeeded in her intention of letting him know that she had no interest in anything more than a close professional relationship?

Or had she—somehow—only succeeded in confirming that any attraction Hawk was experiencing was, indeed, mutual?

CHAPTER SIX

THE backlash was only to be expected.

She deserved it. But Owen Hawkins deserved to suffer as well. How dare he provoke and, yes, dammit, attract her enough to have distracted her from her time of remembrance and personal grief? She hated the man. By the time Charlotte reached the safety of her motel unit she was disgusted with herself. And with Hawk.

How dare he suggest that she should just forget about Jamie and go and find someone else to be the father of her children? He had disparaged the idea that she and Jamie would have been together forever. He had hijacked her grief and shocked her into anger.

No wonder she had been vulnerable to the physical signals he clearly had no compunction in sending her way. That explained the flashes of desire she'd experienced and the appalling temptation to explore them. Thank goodness she hadn't let it go any further. She hadn't really admitted to anything, had she? And if Hawk was assuming she had, she would have no compunction whatsoever in quashing any hopes he might be fostering.

She intended to start first thing the next morning but a sleepless night made it impossible to focus on anything but the job in hand. Her exhaustion prevented any emotion other than the desire to get through the day to surface. Hating someone was out of the question because she was just too damn weary. Fortunately, Hawk didn't present even a glance that needed quashing. It was as though their conversation had never occurred. As though they had never made any kind of footprint on personal ground. It was weird but Charlotte was simply too tired to try and decide whether it made her feel relieved or disappointed that she had not had the chance to make her feelings about him crystal clear.

Charlotte slept on the journey back to the city and she left work with a wave of what was unmistakably relief. She had two days off now unless her pager sounded to signal a job too big for Hawk to handle alone. Laura was also due for her days off. They could get out and enjoy themselves with no male company to create any kind of hassles. Or they could just relax at home. The company of a real friend was just what Charlotte needed at present. She *might* even confess to the possibility of being attracted to Hawk. Laura wouldn't hesitate to convince her what a bizarre notion that was.

Except that Laura wasn't there. She had left a message on the phone to tell Charlotte rather breathlessly that she wouldn't be home that night. She didn't come home the next day until late in the morning and that was only to throw things into a bag. She was a woman on a mission.

'What on earth's going on? Where on earth were you last night?'

'At Jason's house.'

'*What?* Isn't he that fireman who doesn't realise you exist as anything but a paramedic?'

'That's the one.' Laura brushed past Charlotte to head for the bathroom. 'I'd better not forget my toothbrush.'

'You're not moving in with him, are you?'

'Kind of.'

Charlotte followed her friend into the bathroom. 'This is a bit sudden, isn't it? I mean, being attracted to someone is one thing. Dating them is something else. And I don't know what moving in with them out of the blue is!'

'It's not like that.' Laura grinned at Charlotte. 'Jason's got a baby.'

Charlotte could find nothing to say to that.

'He didn't know he had one,' Laura continued happily. 'Until it got left at the fire station for him to take care of. Nobody knows where the mother's gone. Working hours will be OK because Mrs McKendry, who's the housekeeper at the station, has fallen in love with the baby but Jason couldn't possibly cope for the rest of the time.'

'So he's landed you with babysitting?'

'I offered.' Laura pushed her toilet bag into the space in her suitcase. 'She's a really cute baby. Her name's Megan.'

'And she has a really cute father.'

'Who's actually noticed me properly for the first time.'

'As a babysitter?'

'As someone he needs,' Laura corrected. She paused long enough to meet Charlotte's gaze. 'Yeah, I know. I'm probably being used but right now I don't care. I get to be with Jason. To help him. I've never had an opportunity to have anything more than a passing "hello". At least this way we have a chance to get to know each other.'

'How long will you be gone?'

'I have no idea.' Laura sounded remarkably cheerful at the disruption to her life. 'The mother might turn up on the doorstep again any day so I'm just planning to make the most of whatever time I get.' She paused again. 'Will you be OK?'

Charlotte nodded. This was no time to try and discuss any personal issues regarding the man she had to work with. Laura was clearly far too focussed on a different representative of the gender. 'Keep in touch,' she instructed.

'Sure. How did the night with Hawk go, anyway?' Laura was already moving towards the door. 'Did he try and hit on you?'

Charlotte managed a brief but not particularly amused chuckle. 'Not exactly.'

'Just as well for him.' Laura grinned. 'Does he know you used to do martial arts?'

'No.' The thought of trying to protect herself from Hawk physically was a joke anyway. He was a powerful man. He could pursue her and pin her against a wall any time he felt like it.

Good grief! Charlotte watched Laura drive away and tried to berate herself for letting her imagination run wild. Was her body suffering withdrawal symptoms severely enough for her to start having sexual fantasies at the drop of a hat now? Getting pursued and pinned against a wall indeed. To prove how ridiculous it was, Charlotte closed her eyes and actually allowed herself to visualise the scenario. She opened them a few seconds later. That had been a very bad idea. Had her imaginary self been unable...or completely *unwilling* to resist?

A day on her own was also a bad idea. Charlotte did her best to distract herself. She changed into shorts, a singlet top and trainers, and went jogging but it wasn't physical enough. When she reached the bottom of a large hill she stepped up the pace. By the time she reached the top it was painful to try and breathe. Perspiration trickled in uncomfortable rivulets as Charlotte paused and leaned forward, her hands on the railing of someone's fence as she tried to pull in enough oxygen to stop the rest of her body hurting so much.

'Are you all right?'

'Yeah. I'm fine.' Charlotte straightened and smiled at the concerned stranger. She kept to a more moderate pace as she turned for home but she didn't rest when she arrived. Not long after her shower, she was in need of another one, having decided to clean out the old woodshed at the back of Laura's house and chop the pile of wood that was large enough to have been sitting, accumulating spiders and dirt, for a very long time.

She hadn't told the stranger the truth, had she?

She wasn't all right.

'What bothers me more?' she asked a particularly large spider. 'The fact that I'm attracted to Hawk or the fact that I noticed it right at the time I never think of anyone but Jamie?'

The spider vanished under the heap of newly split logs and Charlotte used the axe to lean on. She was physically exhausted again but it wasn't slowing her brain down one little bit.

And how could she have been stupid enough to encourage herself to have some kind of sexual fantasy about the man? She was suffering flashbacks now. Like his face looming closer. When he wasn't looking grim about something or other, Hawk had very soft-looking lips. Mobile. And just full enough for the top one not to disappear when he smiled. What would it feel like if those lips touched her own? To her horror, Charlotte found herself touching her own lips with a gentle brush of a middle finger as the now familiar butterflies beat their wings so hard against the inside of her abdomen it felt almost like a physical pain. She balled her hand into a fist and went inside to have another shower.

'It should be a cold one,' she muttered aloud. The involuntary smile that followed her words was ironic. If someone had told her even a couple of months ago that she would be contemplating a cold shower to distract herself from sexual desire she would have believed herself utterly if she'd reacted by saying something like, 'Not in this life-time.'

Housework couldn't release the tension that Charlotte still needed to get rid of the following day. She vacuumed, she dusted, she cleaned the bathroom. She attacked the linoleum on the kitchen floor with a scrubbing brush and it wasn't until she paused to push damp tendrils of hair away from her face that a vaguely positive thought emerged.

Maybe, just…maybe, this wasn't a bad thing. Charlotte knew about the stages of grief. It had been part of her training as a paramedic. Crash investigators had it as part of their courses as well. Shock and denial were foremost as nature allowed the reality of the loss to sink in slowly. Charlotte had looked and acted like a robot for several days after the news of Jamie's death.

The pain had been unbearable. The tears, anger and even rage had come in waves and had disturbed every aspect of Charlotte's existence. She hadn't eaten or been able to sleep, she'd experienced palpitations and even something that had felt like asthma. The attacks had gone on, intermittently, for months. Then there had been the depression and guilt. The endless 'if onlys'. Jamie *should* have been with her that night. Not out drinking with his mates.

What about idealisation? Charlotte asked herself as she mopped up the last of the soapy water from the floor. Holding to the past and revering it as the best. She knew what the textbooks would say. When energy was locked into the past, there was none available to develop the future. She had moved on, though, and had learned to live with the loss. She still had times of feeling sad but the devastating disruption was over. She was getting on with her life.

Or was she? *Really?* Charlotte emptied the bucket of water and then wandered around the small, quiet house looking for another task. What about those other stages? Like realisation—when you could see the weaknesses in past situations and accept that there was bad as well as good and that you could hope the future would hold good as well as bad. Realising that there was still room for similar things in your life and developing new patterns that allowed their inclusion.

Had she ever reached that stage? Or had she been trapped

by idealisation and been endlessly revisiting previous stages in the cycle to varying degrees without ever taking that final step? It happened often enough but Charlotte wouldn't have believed herself caught. It wasn't that she didn't *want* to find a partner for life. It was lonely enough having two days without Laura in the house. But she had always known that nobody could compete with Jamie, could measure up to everything he had offered both emotionally and physically. Had *that* been some form of denial?

It certainly seemed to be the message her body was trying to convey right now. She wasn't about to have a relationship with Owen Hawkins. Charlotte had been perfectly sincere in saying that her job meant more to her than that. But maybe he had come into her life for a reason. To demonstrate that it was possible for her to feel physically attracted to someone. To show her, finally, that it was time to let go. To start living again. Her body was telling her in no uncertain terms. Perhaps it was time for her heart to give her the freedom to take that step.

It was a big thought. Too much to contemplate other than in small bites. Charlotte couldn't see anything else in the house that needed cleaning. She could go and chop the last pieces of wood but she needed more than spiders for company. She needed something that could jolt her out of this unfamiliar and unwelcome introspection. Going in to work had always been her salvation in the past but that wasn't an option. Hawk was at work and spending time with him right now was something Charlotte really didn't want to deal with. This was all his fault. OK, if this was the point in her life that marked a new start, maybe she would thank him at some point in the future for the emotional turmoil he'd caused. Right now, she still resented it. And him.

The solution was as simple as it was brilliant. Charlotte made some phone calls and an appointment for 7 p.m. that night. She drove a little way out of town, showed the ap-

propriate person her licence and then signed in for thirty
minutes' use of a high-powered gun. She put on her earmuffs and goggles in the cubicle she was allocated, loaded
her gun and checked through the sights to find her target.
The torso-shaped target had circles painted on its chest and
it seemed a long way away. It had been too long since
Charlotte had indulged in the hobby she'd found when doing weapons training for the police force.

Her first shot hit the target's head. At least she hadn't
missed just in case someone was watching. Charlotte carefully avoided catching a glance from anyone into the occupied cubicles on either side and tried to ignore the ache
in her shoulder from the kick of the gun. A muffled shot
came from the person on her left and their target flipped
back out of sight for a second to signify that the bullet had
gone into dead centre of the marked circles. It was a great
shot and Charlotte heard a restrained whoop of delight coming from the marksman. She turned to give her neighbour
a congratulatory smile and the man's eyes widened with
something like alarm beneath the goggles.

'Charlie!'

Lip-reading her own name was easy. Deciding how she
felt about running into Hawk so unexpectedly was rather
more difficult. Charlotte pulled one side of her earmuffs up
as she saw that he was saying something else.

'What?' It was hardly a friendly greeting but Hawk was
smiling.

'I said why didn't you tell me you liked shooting? I come
here all the time and I haven't had anyone to compete with
since Cam left.'

Oh, no! Now she had to prove herself all over again. So
why was she feeling so pleased by the prospect? 'You're
on, buster,' she told Hawk. 'And the loser has to buy the
beer.'

Charlotte lost but only just. Her aim improved steadily

until she was hitting the central mark just as often as Hawk but she couldn't make up the lost ground.

'Your shout,' he informed her smugly as they handed back their weapons. 'I like beer.'

'You're on call,' Charlotte reminded him. 'You'll have to take a rain-check. And it's just as well because I'm not used to this any more. I've got a thundering headache and a very sore shoulder. I'm going to head home for a long soak in a hot bath.'

Hawk was keeping pace with her as she headed for her car. 'Are you in a huge hurry?'

'Why?'

'There's something I'd like to show you.'

An odd note in Hawk's tone earned him a sharp glance. 'What? Have I done something wrong?'

'No, it's nothing to do with your work. Not in that sense, anyway.'

Now Charlotte was curious. 'What is it, then?'

'Can't say,' Hawk said firmly. 'It's something you've got to see.'

The lure of the hot bath receded just a little. 'Will it take long?'

'Nope. Couple of minutes. And it's practically on your way home.'

'I don't believe it.' Charlotte could only stare at what was sitting on top of her desk.

'Don't worry, you can mess things up again. I just cleared a small space.'

But it wasn't a small thing. It was huge. Charlotte found she had a lump in her throat and she had to swallow. She glanced up to find Hawk watching her carefully. His expression advertised pride and something a lot more than that. He had done something for *her* and he wanted her to be pleased.

Charlotte was more than pleased. She was blown away.

'I don't believe it,' she repeated slowly. 'This must have cost an absolute fortune, Hawk!'

'It did.' Hawk tried to sound modest but his face was a dead give-away. 'I had a few words in the right ears. You would have enjoyed the yarn I spun about poor Stan Jones. The benefits to public relations for the police force did not go unmentioned either.'

'But…' Charlotte couldn't resist touching it now, and once she started, she couldn't stop. 'This is state of the art, Hawk. It's got *everything*!' She unzipped pockets on the carry case one after the other and then she turned the machine on and found a menu screen. She shook her head as she scrolled through the options.

'Twelve lead ECG, pacing capabilities, non-invasive blood-pressure measurement, oximeter, end-tidal carbon dioxide. It's even got rhythm analysis.'

'I have no idea what all that stuff means,' Hawk confessed cheerfully.

'It means that we've got a life pack that's probably better than most of the ambulances in the district carry.'

'Good.' Hawk sounded smug. 'I only pick the best.'

'But…' Charlotte was still stunned. 'How often are we going to use it?'

'How much is a life worth?' Hawk countered. His gaze held something indefinable now. 'Some people are worth whatever it costs,' he added softly.

Charlotte had to look away. Was he talking about potential heart-attack victims? Or was he referring to how much money had just been spent on *her* behalf? A wave of confusion made her stammer a little.

'H-how on earth are we going to fit this into our car?'

'We'll manage.' Hawk was fiddling with some files lying beside the life pack on Charlotte's desk. 'So…what do you think?' The edge of a file pushed the vase of fake flower pens and Jamie's photograph tipped over to lie face down.

And Charlotte wasn't even tempted to reach out and pick it up. 'I think it's the most amazing thing anyone's ever done for me, Hawk.' She cleared her throat. 'Thank you.'

There was a moment of silence. An awkward one. If it had been anyone other than Hawk, Charlotte would not have hesitated to give him a hug. But there was no way she could *hug* Owen Hawkins. It wouldn't be a friendly gesture of appreciation. It would be something far more dangerous. She didn't want to touch this man.

She didn't dare.

'You're welcome.' Hawk straightened from where he'd been leaning on her desk beside the life pack. He sounded as awkward as Charlotte felt. 'Uh…there was something else as well. A favour I wanted to ask.'

'Ah!' Charlotte tried to recapture some of their usual professional tension. 'I might have known there was a catch.'

Hawk's smile was brief. 'I wanted to ask you if you could teach me to do CPR properly.'

'Oh…' Charlotte hadn't expected that. Hawk wanted something that she could give him? He certainly deserved it. 'But there are courses you could go on,' she found herself saying. 'You could get a qualification if you wanted to.'

'I don't want to,' Hawk said simply. 'I want *you* to teach me.'

'No problem, then,' Charlotte said. 'I'd be happy to teach you, Hawk. I should be able to rustle up a dummy through Laura.'

'We'd have to find our own time to do it. Evenings, probably.'

Charlotte had to wet suddenly dry lips. 'No problem.' She had to clear her throat again. 'It's a great idea, Hawk.

And there's heaps you can learn. Like paediatric resuscitation. A cardiac arrest in a child is often caused by a respiratory arrest happening first, which is different to adults. Potentially, you could have a child with an obstructed airway leading to an arrest at an accident scene that could be saved by good CPR.' She was babbling. It was time she left.

A riot of conflicting emotions were trying to gain precedence over each other. Had she really thought she hated Hawk only two days ago? A tiny task that presented itself as a distraction was welcome. Charlotte leaned over her desk and stood Jamie's photograph upright again. By the time she looked up, Hawk had moved. He was returning to his desk despite it being long after his official knocking off time.

'I'll look forward to it,' he said politely. 'But right now I've got a report I want to get finished.'

'I'll get out of your way, then,' Charlotte told him. She paused at the door. 'Thanks again, Hawk.'

'You're welcome.' Hawk still sounded oddly polite.

'I hope we get a chance to play with it soon. Kind of,' she added. What would Hawk think if he knew she was looking forward to another situation like Mr Jones had caused? 'Not that it's likely,' she continued. 'I haven't had a chance for much fluffing lately, have I?'

'No.' Hawk smiled but his gaze remained on his computer screen. 'Still, you never know what's around the corner, do you?' He wasn't expecting a response. His fingers were busily tapping keys already.

Charlotte took the hint and fled.

Her dreams that night were a jigsaw of medical emergencies. Hawk was present in more than one of them, carrying a life-saving defibrillator that filled Charlotte with an overwhelming sense of relief. There were snatches of other overwhelming emotions concerning Owen Hawkins as well, yet Charlotte felt that she had slept well for the first time in many days. She awoke to find the tension had gone. She felt rested, calm and ready for anything. She was looking forward to getting back to work today.

It was just as well she had recharged her batteries. She needed every ounce of energy and alertness she could summon when she and Hawk were despatched that afternoon to another major incident.

'What is it with us and trucks lately?' Charlotte had to raise her voice over the sound of the siren as they sped towards the outskirts of the city.

'They're big and heavy. They tend to squash things they hit.'

'And they use up too much of the road. Like that sheep truck—it was halfway into the car's lane.' Charlotte slowed the car a little as they approached a bend. 'How many vehicles has this one collected?'

'It's squashed one under the front and a couple of others have piled into the back of it.'

A fine, misty rain had made road conditions slippery. Failing to heed the speed the advisory sign recommended for taking a bend in such conditions, a car had skidded, turned clockwise 180 degrees and ended up in the lane of opposing traffic. A truck driver had done his best to brake but had been unable to prevent the collision. His front wheels had gone over the back of the car, crushing the left-hand side beneath the heavy vehicle, and had then shunted it some distance along the road. Another car had crashed into the rear of a bus as it had braked and they in turn had been rear-ended by a delivery van.

The scene was chaotic. Injured car passengers included a couple of hysterical teenage girls. The driver of the car under the front of the furniture truck was still alive but badly injured, and it had taken some time for the fire service to cut access to the victim. Her passenger would have to remain where he was, buried in the crushed side of the car still under the wheels of the truck. The ambulance service was stretched to deal with the multi-casualty incident and Hawk took one look at the scene as they arrived and turned to Charlotte.

'See where you're needed most,' he told her. 'I'll start the scene investigation.'

Charlotte was needed most at the car. She found Laura trying to stabilise the critically injured driver and she was clearly having difficulty. The suction gear beside her was full of blood. A discarded endotracheal tube was also covered in blood and Laura was holding a smaller size of tube as she peered past the light her laryngoscope provided.

'I can't see a thing,' she was saying in dismay. 'And there's no way I can get even this tube in. Her trachea's crushed.'

The stridor Charlotte could hear as the injured woman struggled to breathe was alarming. If they couldn't achieve some airway protection there was no way they could keep her alive long enough to reach the hospital. A rescue helicopter with further back-up was approaching to land just over the road in the vacant parking lot of a factory but it would take several minutes for them to be able to offer assistance.

Laura's partner was someone Charlotte didn't recognise and he was less qualified than Tim. He shook his head as he held the bag mask over the patient's face again.

'I'm not getting any air in,' he said grimly. 'Her airway's totally obstructed.' He reached for the suction unit again and inserted the end piece into the woman's mouth. A fresh flow of blood entered the tubing to take the level in the reservoir up with alarming speed.

'Try a cricothyroid puncture,' Charlotte advised Laura.

'I've never done one.' Laura bit her lip. 'Not for real.'

'I'm not even qualified to try.' Tim's replacement for the shift sounded equally anxious.

They both looked at Charlotte. 'I've done a few,' she admitted. 'OK. I'll have one more go at intubation and if that fails we'll go for a cric.'

Hawk passed close to the trio of ambulance officers a minute or so later. He could see that the situation was extremely tense and he heard Charlotte sounding very grim.

'There's subcutaneous emphysema all over her neck. Hand me that 12-gauge cannula, Laura. Have you attached the 10 mil syringe with 3 mil of saline in it?'

'Yes.' Laura sounded as though she had supreme confidence in what Charlotte was doing. 'Here you go.'

Hawk stopped dead in his tracks as he *saw* what Charlotte was doing. She had already been feeling the patient's neck carefully. Now she was pushing the large needle directly into the front of the woman's neck.

'I'm aspirating with the syringe as I go,' he heard her say to her companions. 'I'll either aspirate air bubbles or blood or I'll feel a break in resistance as I cross the tracheal wall.'

Hawk couldn't move. The next few seconds were far too tense.

'Yes!' Charlotte sounded delighted. 'Air bubbles. Now I'm advancing the cannula and we'll confirm placement with an empty syringe.'

'What size?' Laura's hand hovered over the kit close to Charlotte as she knelt beside the unconscious woman.

'Another 10 will be fine. Have you got that Y-connector attached to the oxygen tubing, Pete?'

'All set to go. Fifteen litres?'

'Yep.' Charlotte reached for the new gear. 'Let's get some air into her.'

The helicopter had landed by now and brightly suited

and helmeted paramedics were advancing on the scene, rolling a stretcher between them. Hawk moved away. There was no room for extra bodies in this area and too much for him to do elsewhere. He was surprised when Charlotte joined him a minute later. A few spots of blood on her white shirt were the only indications of the dramatic procedure she had just completed.

'It's under control,' she told Hawk. 'They're just getting her packaged for transport. There's only minor stuff from the other vehicles and there'll be plenty of ambulance staff to deal with them once the chopper gets away. I'm all yours.'

He wished.

'What were you doing to that woman?' Hawk needed to dispel that errant thought as quickly as possible. 'It looked pretty serious.'

'It was. She was already hypovolaemic from her injuries and she would have died from hypoxia pretty damned quickly if we hadn't done something.'

Hawk gave Charlotte a blank look and she smiled. 'Sorry. Serious blood loss and lack of oxygen. She'd crushed her trachea…' Charlotte stroked the front of her own neck to indicate the area she was talking about. 'There was no way we could get a tube in to get her breathing properly because there was too much tissue damage and bleeding. The obstruction was enough to make using a bag mask ineffective as well.'

Hawk was finding it difficult to concentrate on what she was saying. He was still staring at her neck. He wanted to stroke it himself. Shaking his head to clear the increasingly unwelcome distractions, he moved off. Charlotte kept pace with him as he marched along the road.

'What I did was a needle cricothyroidotomy. It's like a temporary tracheotomy. Even a needle can allow enough oxygen to get in under pressure to keep someone alive long enough to do a proper surgical airway.'

'That's cool.' Hawk was focussed again now. He wasn't even annoyed with himself any more. The distraction of his desire for Charlotte had been only momentary. A brief flash that could be put aside until a more suitable time.

'Look at that.' A learner's plate card was lying on the road surface not far from the woman's car. 'She was driving, wasn't she?'

'Yep.' Charlotte shook her head. 'Her passenger isn't going anywhere and he certainly didn't have a chance to change seats.'

'Friction marks,' Hawk pointed out. The lines wiggled in a bizarre pattern. 'The car's been shunted. They're post-impact marks.'

Charlotte nodded. She turned her head for a moment to watch the helicopter take off.

'We'll have to get a crane in to lift the truck off the car. We're going to be here for a while.'

Charlotte nodded again. 'I'll get the paint and my sketch book.'

It was well over an hour before the truck got lifted from the car and then towed away. The total devastation of the vehicle provoked a soft curse from Hawk. The steering-wheel of the truck had been directly over the passenger seat of the car. The windscreen and roof of the vehicle were flattened to the same level as the bonnet on that side. The body of the passenger was barely visible amidst the crushed metal and it took the fire service another thirty minutes to extricate the body of the unfortunate man.

Then the wreck could be lifted by the crane and both Hawk and Charlotte peered at the underside of the car.

'There's severe rim damage on the front right wheel.'

Hawk nodded. 'And look at this scraping under the petrol

tank. You're lucky we didn't have a fire while you were trying to work beside it.'

'I doubt that a fire would have lasted long in this weather. Freezing, isn't it?'

'We've got just about enough information for now. Let's get back to the office and see what we're missing. I think anything else we're going to need will still be here in the morning.'

Reviewing all the digital photographs on the computer was the last task they did that day but it was well past the time they should have gone home, and their office was an oasis of light in an otherwise dark department. Charlotte stretched her shoulders back as she sat in front of the computer. Then she rubbed her shoulder.

'I'm beginning to wish I hadn't taken you up on that challenge at the rifle range yesterday.'

'That's just because you still owe me those beers.' Hawk was standing behind her. He watched her rubbing her shoulder. Then, almost without thinking, he placed his own hands on Charlotte's shoulders.

'Now, *that's* something *I* can cure,' he informed her.

His fingers anchored themselves above her collarbones while his thumbs kneaded the muscles on either side of the base of her neck. He increased the pressure gradually and Charlotte groaned.

'Oh…yes! That's the spot. Ouch! Are you sure you know what you're doing, Hawk?'

'Oh, yes. I'm sure.'

But he wasn't. He was good at giving neck and shoulder massages but what he was doing right now was probably a big mistake. He had his hands on Charlotte Laing and the messages his fingers were relaying to his brain—not to mention other parts of his anatomy—had very little to do with anything therapeutic.

Charlotte had become very still and quiet, and Hawk

found the movement of his hands slowing. He dropped them to the back of her swivel chair and found himself turning her to face him. The expression on her face made him wonder whether the physical contact had had just as disturbing an effect on her as it was having on him.

She sat looking up at him with a vaguely dreamy expression clouding her eyes. Her lips were slightly parted and it was the sight of the pink tongue tip that was Hawk's complete undoing. He had to lean down a long way to reach Charlotte's mouth with his own but within seconds he was no longer stooping. Had he dragged Charlotte up to her feet or had she risen to follow his lips? It didn't matter. The movement and the contact were so seamless he couldn't tell where his own body finished and Charlotte's started.

And he had never, ever experienced a kiss anything like this one. He was in danger of drowning in the flood of sensation it provoked. Or suffocating because his body would not obey his brain and come up for air.

Charlotte was equally breathless when she finally pulled away. Her gaze was as wild as the desire still building in Hawk.

'This isn't going to happen, Hawk.' The words were punctuated with a gasp for air. 'It *can't* happen.'

Hawk caught her shoulders again but this time he didn't pull her towards him. He knew she would resist, and trying to persuade her by physical means would spell definite failure. Instead, he spoke softly.

'Jamie's not here any more, Charlie, and I'm sorry about that for your sake.' He wasn't sorry for his own sake. No way. 'But you can't lock all that passion away. Something inside you is going to wither and die if you deny it for too long. You'll end up with only half a life.' His fingers eased their hold and then squeezed again gently.

'I'm here,' he whispered. 'I want you, Charlie. More than I've ever wanted any woman.' His gaze locked with

Charlotte's. 'And if that kiss is anything to go by, I think you want me, too.'

Charlotte shook her head but Hawk wasn't going to give up just yet. 'You need to start living again.' His smile felt curiously crooked. 'And I'd like to be the person you start your new life with.'

'It's not going to happen, Hawk.' Charlotte pulled away. In an instant she had grabbed her bag and in another she was gone, with the echo of her words following her. 'It can't.'

Hawk was left standing in the office with only the memory of that kiss.

'Oh, it's going to happen,' he murmured. 'It's just a question of *when*, Charlotte Laing. Not *if*.'

CHAPTER SEVEN

'I HATE these jobs.'

'Hit and runs?' Charlotte glanced up only briefly from the map she was consulting. 'Take the next left, Hawk. McGuire's Road.'

Hawk slowed down a little. The blue and red beacons of the squad car were flashing but the siren was silent. The lights were enough to warn any other traffic on the dark roads of a quiet rural area.

'Some bastard clipped someone walking down the side of the road and just kept going.'

'Maybe he thought he'd hit a sheep or something.'

Hawk didn't seem to have heard her. 'Or, worse, maybe he stopped and had a look and then got back into his car and took off.'

'Panic can make people do things they otherwise wouldn't.'

'Ha!' Clearly, Hawk wasn't going to find any excuse plausible.

'I feel sorry for the person who ran over the victim later.' Charlotte shook her head as she sighed. 'He had no chance of avoiding a body lying in the middle of the road.'

'He could have still been alive until that second vehicle got him.'

Charlotte could see Hawk's knuckles, pale against the dark steering-wheel. She could imagine the tension in his hands...how tight the grip was. She tried to concentrate on the map again. Hawk's hands were becoming an obsession.

Ever since he'd kissed her—three days ago now—she had been at pains to avoid any length of eye contact or the temptation to watch his mouth when he spoke, but that meant her gaze invariably settled on his hands. Charlotte would recognise those hands in isolation anywhere now, and she could have drawn them quite accurately from memory had she any inclination to do so. She knew the length of his fingers, the shape of his nails, that scar on the third knuckle of his left hand that looked like a tiny fork of lightning. She knew the way they moved when he picked something up, the way they held a pen and the way Hawk used them to massage his forehead when he was ill at ease about something. She also knew, thanks to that shoulder massage and...and *that* kiss, the sensations those hands were capable of evoking in her.

And that was driving her nuts. It had only been a massage. The kind of physical contact any friends, or colleagues, could indulge in. OK, the kiss had been more than that. A hell of a lot more but Charlotte knew beyond a shadow of doubt that there was still a lot she *didn't* know about what those hands could do. For three nights now she had done her best *not* to imagine what sensations they might conjure up by touching her breasts, stroking that spot on her inner thighs or actually...

'Have they moved the body yet?' The question came out very abruptly but Charlotte had to keep her mind on the job somehow.

'Not yet.' Hawk's response was equally terse. 'They're waiting for us to check the scene.'

'We're not too far away, now.' Charlotte was keeping her gaze and her mind firmly on the map she held. 'We should be there in ten minutes or so.'

It didn't help that it was nearly 10 p.m. and the call from home which meant they would be spending extra time together had been unexpected. It was a forty-minute drive at high speed into an isolated rural area. The return trip at normal road speed would take a lot longer but it was still not far enough away to warrant having to stay overnight close to the scene.

The thought that it *could* have been had been disturbing enough when the call had come in. Sometime, probably in the not-too-distant future, they would be stuck overnight in some motel. The opportunity to satisfy her curiosity would be there again and Charlotte was beginning to seriously doubt any ability she had to resist the temptation.

And why should she? They were both adults. They were both quite capable of knowing what they wanted. And what they didn't want. If they wanted to play—out of sight or knowledge of anyone who might disapprove on a professional level—then why not? Did Hawk still want to? Charlotte had been so careful to avoid any communication, spoken or otherwise, that could be misinterpreted she had no idea what Hawk might be thinking. She had been very definite that nothing was going to happen between them when she'd walked out after that kiss, and he'd said nothing in the last few days to make her think that her edict was about to be challenged in any way.

Surely Hawk hadn't given up that easily?

Only three vehicles marked the whereabouts of the fatal incident but the flashing beacons of the local police officer's car made it visible several kilometres down the long, straight road. Hawk was aware of a vague sense of disappointment in locating the scene. If only this job had been a bit further away, they would have had to stay the night somewhere. Hawk would have given rather a lot to add another thirty kilometres or so to their journey at that point. The thought of how different things might have been gave him cause to suppress a small smile.

Charlotte had been so busy being careful to avoid giving him any encouragement for the last three days, she had made it as obvious as a neon sign that she was thinking about him just as much as he was about her. If she had carried on as normal, he might have given up any hope of winning this challenge. If she'd been able to brush that kiss aside and not let it make any difference to the way they interacted, then he would have known she wasn't interested. Charlotte probably imagined she was playing it cool but Hawk was quite sure that the effects of that kiss had lingered on both sides. He was perfectly confident in his opinion that it was a matter of *when* and not *if*—but it wasn't going to be tonight, dammit!

Another vehicle could be seen approaching from the opposite direction, a sleek, dark station wagon that had to be a hearse. The reminder that the covered shape they could see as Hawk pulled to a halt was the innocent victim of a hit and run was enough to pull his mind back to the job at hand. This was no time to indulge in any fantasies of what he would do if…no, *when*, he got Charlotte into his bedroom. No doubt the drive home would be harder to cope with but for now it was easy to file the whole issue under the same category as other pleasurable activities for out-of-work hours. Like squash and target shooting. They had an unpleasant job to get on with here and the sooner it was completed, the better.

It was easy enough to begin with.

'I'll see what information I can get about the injuries to the victim,' Charlotte offered. 'Unless you want to?'

Hawk shook his head. Charlotte was far more qualified than he was to make sense of whatever she found out. He stayed where he was to continue the discussion with the local police officers.

'Where's the driver who called in the incident?'

'Down at Maggie's. He's having a cup of tea.' The senior constable was fishing a notebook from his pocket. 'His name's Ivan Colleridge. We've got all his details and a statement, here.'

'What did he have to say?'

'That he didn't see anything. He slammed on his brakes after the bump and then didn't think to shift it before he ran for help.' He waved a hand at the stationary vehicle still on the road on the other side of the victim. 'It's lucky nobody ran into his car when he went off and left it like that.'

'There was no coverage for his cellphone here,' the junior officer added.

Hawk had already noted another set of brake marks. On *his* side of the victim. Whoever had clipped the pedestrian had at least made an attempt to stop. Had that been before or after the impact? Hawk returned his gaze to his companions.

'Who's Maggie?'

'Maggie Shaw,' he was informed. 'She used to be a nurse. Mr Colleridge went in to use her phone after the accident and she came out to see if she could do anything. She says Jim was stone cold. She reckons he'd been dead for quite a while.'

Hawk just made a mental note of the information. Charlotte would probably be able to estimate time of death. He could see her out of the corner of his eye. The cover had been removed from the body and Maggie was wearing gloves, obviously checking the injuries being described by the paramedics holding torches beside her. The crew of the hearse were standing at a discreet distance, their trolley prepared and their protective gloves and plastic aprons reflecting a glimmer of the faint moonlight.

'We'll need to talk to them both,' Hawk said.

'They're not far away. Maggie's house is just up the road a bit. Huge old house—one of the original homesteads around here. She runs a homestay business these days. Bed and breakfast, you know?'

Hawk nodded. 'Did she notice anything unusual earlier this evening?'

'She reckons she heard *something*. And her dogs were kicking up a bit of racket about eight o'clock but she's rather hard of hearing and she was a bit upset herself after finding Jimmy.'

'The victim?'

'Yeah. His name's Jim Patterson but everybody calls him Jimmy. He's a bit of a local character, really. He's got himself into more than one scrape over the years and this won't be the first time he forgot to fill up and ran out of petrol on his way back from town.'

'He'd forget his head if it wasn't screwed on.' The younger officer's grin faded rapidly after an admonishing glance from his senior colleague.

'So where's his car?'

'About two kilometres down the road. You must have passed it.'

Hawk blinked. Had he been so preoccupied with thoughts of the woman sitting beside him that he could have let a major piece of evidence like that go unnoticed? And why hadn't Charlotte spotted an abandoned vehicle? What had *she* been thinking about?

'Easy to miss,' the local police officer said kindly. 'It's well onto the verge and it looks like a wreck, anyway.'

'You sure it's Mr Patterson's car?'

'Oh, yeah. I had to write him out a ticket for not having a warrant only last week. He said he forgot but I'd re-minded him more than once in the last three months.'

'And the petrol tank is empty?'

'Yep. His petrol can's on the side of the road in the grass. We haven't moved anything. Want me to show you where it is?'

'Thanks, but I'll find it. The fewer people walking

around the scene the better from now on. There could be other important evidence that shouldn't be disturbed.'

'There's only been me and Will, apart from the ambulance guys. And Mr Colleridge and Maggie, I guess.' The officer looked sideways to where the staff from the funeral home were transferring the body to the hearse. 'And them,' he added slowly. He shook his head sadly. 'Poor old Jimmy. Place won't be the same without him. ''Specially the pub.'

'Did he drink a lot?'

'Nah. That was where he went for company. He could nurse the same pint for hours.'

'Unless someone bought him one,' his colleague added. 'Then he'd finish his own in a flash.'

Hawk made another note. If the victim had been intoxicated he might well have wandered away from the safety of the wide grass verge. Not that that could excuse the driver who had hit him initially for not stopping to render assistance. It was not just illegal to leave the scene of an accident. It was downright immoral and Hawk was determined that the offender would be brought to justice, no matter how difficult that might prove to be.

Charlotte had marked the position of the body carefully before it had been removed.

'He definitely wasn't killed by the second vehicle,' she informed Hawk. 'Track marks over both legs but it was the chest and head injuries that were fatal.'

'How long ago?'

'I'm no expert. I was talking about it with the paramedic who filled in the ''life extinct'' form, though, and we think it was at least a couple of hours ago.'

'There's a petrol can in the long grass over there, apparently. He was on his way to get some fuel.'

'So where's his car?'

'We passed it a couple of kilometres back from the scene.'

'Did we?'

Charlotte's eyes were wide as her gaze caught Hawk's, and his resolve to keep his obsession well away from the job went out the window. Even in this dim light the flash of guilt in the depths of her eyes let him know that she had been preoccupied for exactly the same reason he had been. He tucked that piece of information into the mental file that should be remaining firmly closed as he turned to go and locate the position of the petrol can. It could be the most important clue they had in relation to whether the driver of the offending vehicle had seen the victim before hitting him.

'Just once,' he found himself muttering under his breath. That would be enough to stop himself getting distracted like this. Just one night with Charlotte Laing and he could get her out of his system, he was sure of it. This was a physical obsession. He knew he'd never be able to compete with the ghost of Jamie Forrest and he didn't want to. It made Charlotte even more attractive in a way.

Hawk had no desire to make himself vulnerable to the emotional tentacles a long-term relationship sent out. He just wanted to satisfy his curiosity, that was all. She was so unlike any woman he'd ever known. All he needed to do was prove it was not really so different between the sheets and he'd get over it. It was the curiosity that was eating him alive. Wanting to know what it would be like.

Wanting Charlotte.

He could have found out tonight if only they'd been a bit further out of town. Shame the car was maintained so well. No chance of them running out of petrol like poor old Jimmy. Although there was always the kill switch under the dashboard which prevented the car being started even if the keys were left in the ignition. Would Charlotte think to check that if they were last on scene and the squad car refused to start?

Probably. And it was pointless to scheme in any case. The scene would have to be protected overnight and they were close enough to the city for assistance to be despatched if it was deemed necessary. Hawk's breath was expelled in a heavy sigh as he sprayed fluorescent paint around the petrol can to mark the piece of evidence and then straightened to see what Charlotte was up to.

They spent another thirty minutes on scene and Charlotte was excited by the latest evidence the beams from their powerful torches had revealed.

'There's heaps of pieces from an indicator light. Have you checked the second car?'

'It's not damaged.'

'Look!' Charlotte held up a piece of coloured plastic, using the beam of her torch as a pointer. 'This bit's got part of a serial number.' The torch raked the rest of the scattered shards still lying on the tarmac. 'If we can find the rest of the number, it'll give us the make and approximate year of the vehicle we're hunting for.'

'We can't search properly until daylight. We'll have to leave everything as it is until then.'

The reminder that they needed to drive back to the city was unwelcome. They should be staying—at least close to the scene. Like at a motel…Charlotte bit her lip and tried to concentrate. On the job, she told herself firmly, not on inventing some reason to detain them.

'But that's wasting time. This car might have a broken windscreen as well as the indicator light and they'll need to stop and get that fixed. If the victim was hit with enough force to smash the light it could well have knocked off a side mirror as well. Let's keep hunting, Hawk. A mirror would give us the colour of the car and we could have garages warned to keep a look out.'

'There's not many garages open after midnight. We can't do anything more right now. We might well ruin some evidence by stomping all over it in the dark.'

Charlotte's acceptance of the inevitable was grudging. 'The scene needs protecting, then.'

'The local guys have got that covered.'

'Oh. So I guess we're heading back to town?'

'No. We're going to talk to Maggie.'

'The nurse, right?' Ivan Colleridge had already returned to the scene, spoken at length to the police and been taken back to the city by another police vehicle. His own car would have to be examined the following day by forensic experts before it could be completely cleared of having caused the fatal injuries to the victim. 'It's getting a bit late, isn't it, Hawk?' Charlotte checked her watch and tried not to sound too pleased at the delay. 'It's nearly 1 a.m.'

'She's expecting us. She runs a B&B so she's probably used to being disturbed at odd hours.'

A B&B was almost the same as a motel. Charlotte found herself almost hoping that the squad car would refuse to start when Hawk turned the key, then they would have an excuse not to try and get back to town that night. But it started first go, of course, and that was probably just as well. This was simply a physical obsession and she had to find a way to cope with it and move on.

It was time she moved on. Time to see whether it was possible to add that missing dimension to her life. It wasn't being disloyal to Jamie. Charlotte could be quite certain that Jamie wouldn't have remained celibate if she had vanished from *his* life. And maybe Hawk was right. Maybe he was the perfect partner to start with. He wasn't going to push her in any direction she didn't want to go. He didn't want any kind of long-term relationship. And he hated kids.

Look at the way he'd reacted to Cam's news. Only yesterday he had announced that he wasn't going to make any attempt to get to the States for the wedding, which was only a few weeks away.

This was purely physical and it didn't need to be a big deal. One night would be enough. Just finding out whether she was capable of physical satisfaction again would let her know that she was taking the right path here. She was sure Hawk would oblige, providing the circumstances were right. And he was an ideal candidate quite apart from his aversion to involvement. He was probably very good in bed. With everything he had going for him, he must have clocked up plenty of practice by now.

The circumstances weren't going to be right tonight, however, and Charlotte followed her partner up the steps and onto the verandah of the large old house with a weariness of spirit that was suddenly competing with the increasing tiredness of her body.

Maggie Shaw was certainly expecting the visit.

'Do come in,' she urged, after they had introduced themselves. 'I've got a nice hot cup of tea waiting for you. You must be exhausted.' Pushing half-moon spectacles back into position on the bridge of her nose, she immediately dislodged them again by shaking her head. 'Such a terrible job you have to do but I suppose someone has to.' She peered at Maggie. 'I wasn't expecting a young girl like you, though, dear.'

'Thank you for seeing us, Mrs Shaw. We'll try not to take up too much of your time.'

Maggie didn't appear to have heard Charlotte. Shadowed by two obedient border collies, she led the way through an impressively tiled foyer, past a gracefully curving stairway and down a hallway that led to a vast kitchen where an ancient coal range sat surprisingly juxtaposed to the latest in European cookware. She still hadn't stopped talking by the time she ushered Hawk and Charlotte onto chairs around a scrubbed pine table.

'I mean, he *was* pushing seventy, I suppose, but there was still a lot of life in Jimmy. He was supposed to come and help me with my redecoration next week. I've had all six bedrooms emptied so I can get them repainted. Goodness knows how I'll cope now. Still, I expect I'll manage somehow.'

'So you're on your own here at present?' Any hope of finding a witness who might be able to help in the investigation faded.

'Presents? It's far too soon to start thinking about Christmas.' Maggie glanced up from her task of pouring hot water into a silver teapot to catch two blank expressions. 'Sorry. I'm as deaf as a post. You'll have to speak up a bit, dear.'

Charlotte caught a faintly amused glance from Hawk as she raised her voice. 'You don't have any guests staying at the moment?'

'No. Nowhere to put them until I get the painting done. Except for the old sod cottage in the orchard and that's not to everybody's taste. Very original but quaint. There's two bedrooms but only one loo and it's a long walk from the main house in the dark.'

It sounded rather inviting to Charlotte. She avoided meeting Hawk's eye as she gratefully accepted the steaming china cup of tea.

'How was Mr Colleridge when he was here?' Hawk asked.

'Who?'

'Mr Colleridge. The man who came to use your phone.'

'Oh…Ivan. He was in a dreadful state, poor man. And who wouldn't be? He thought he'd just killed someone after all. So did I, to be honest, until I realised that poor Jimmy had actually been dead for quite a while.' Maggie peered over her spectacles. 'It's a long time since I was a nurse but I do remember what dead bodies are like and he wasn't...fresh, if you know what I mean.'

Charlotte nodded and disguised the twitch of her lips by taking a sip of tea.

'It's not as though Jimmy was a pillar of society or anything but he was one of us. He probably wouldn't have remembered to turn up to help me next week but we *liked* him despite his faults. He didn't deserve to die like that.' Maggie pushed a plate of home-made biscuits towards her guests. She clucked disapprovingly a moment later but it wasn't due to her offering being declined. 'It's such a dreadful thing to have done, isn't it? To hit someone and simply drive away. I can't understand it at all. I do hope you catch whoever did this.'

'We intend to,' Hawk said grimly. 'We'll be back first thing in the morning to carry on our investigation.'

'Oh, you're not going to drive all the way to town at this hour, are you? That's ridiculous. You'll have no sleep at all to speak of.'

'We're used to it,' Charlotte assured her. 'We'll manage.'

'But you don't need to,' Maggie protested. 'I can't offer you any of the good rooms but the cottage is perfectly habitable.' She smiled at Hawk. 'You and Mrs Hawkins would be quite comfortable.' Hawk's expression made her blink. 'You *are* married, aren't you, dears?'

'No.' Hawk and Charlotte's hurried response was simultaneous.

'Really?' Maggie blinked again. 'Funny, I thought you must be. You seem so...' She clicked her tongue. 'There I go again. Mad old Maggie.' A cheerful smile appeared. 'There *are* two bedrooms in the cottage. Are you friendly enough to share a bathroom?'

Charlotte kept her eyes resolutely on the plate of chocolate-chip biscuits. She could feel her heart racing uncomfortably. Here it was, an unexpected opportunity being offered. Nobody would have to know what actually went on in that cottage. Except for her and Hawk.

'Of course we are.' Hawk's voice sounded a trifle strained and he cleared his throat. 'It does seem more sensible than driving home for a few hours' sleep, doesn't it, Charlie?'

This was it. If she didn't want time alone with Hawk, with all the possibilities that presented, then she would have to say something. Now.

'Mmm.' As an articulate response it really didn't rate but the effect was startling.

'That's settled, then.' Maggie beamed. 'I'm so glad I can do something really useful. I'll find some towels and show you the way.'

Hawk said nothing aloud but the look he gave Charlotte spoke volumes. She found her knees curiously weak as she stood up to follow their now bustling hostess.

The cottage was a delight. The thick walls, low, beamed ceilings and soft lighting from imitation hurricane lamps gave it an instantly welcoming feel. Hawk and Charlotte wandered around again after Maggie had finally left, having given firm instructions to come up to the main house for breakfast. Not that there was much to explore. A small living room with an open fireplace, a tiny bathroom and two bedrooms, one of which had an old, single brass bedstead while the other was almost entirely filled by a beautiful, wooden four-poster bed. A double bed. Charlotte was still admiring the detailed carving of flowers adorning the posts when she realised that Hawk was repeating what he'd said.

'I said, which bed do you fancy?'

Charlotte grinned. 'There's not much of a contest, is there? I'd like this one.'

Hawk's gaze caught hers. 'So would I,' he said softly.

Charlotte had to bite her lip to prevent a nervous squeak escaping. Hawk was standing very close to her. She could feel the heat his body was generating. Or was it electricity? Something had instantly charged the atmosphere to an almost unbearable level of tension. She had to say something.

'Shall we toss a coin?'

Hawk didn't appear to share any of her nerves, and why should he? The question had already been asked after all. She'd had her chance to back out when Maggie had first suggested they stay in the cottage together.

'Maybe we could share.' And Hawk smiled as his gaze still remained locked on hers.

The eye contact seemed to go on forever but Charlotte couldn't look away. She was mesmerised. She remained completely immobilised as Hawk reached out and traced the outlines of her face with his fingers. The contact left a trail of fire across her temple and cheekbone, then down the side of her nose. Charlotte closed her eyes and sighed softly at the touch on her lower lip. Unconsciously, her lips parted, allowing her tongue to touch the gently exploring finger.

Now it was Hawk's turn to pause and emit a soft sound of need. The hesitation was only momentary—a punctuation mark as his lips took the place of that solitary finger. Lips as gentle as the touch of his hand had been until, again, Charlotte used the tip of her tongue in response.

She had to wind her arms around Hawk's neck then to steady herself under the passionate onslaught of the kiss. And even that measure was inadequate. Charlotte could feel his hands slipping beneath her shirt, sliding up the bare skin of her back, keeping her upright as she stumbled backwards. A flash of that fantasy of Hawk pursuing her and pinning her to a wall surfaced, and now Charlotte knew that it was definitely unwillingness rather than inability that made her powerless to prevent what was happening. And this was *so* much more exciting than any fantasy.

Not even such a lengthy abstinence could take the credit for making her body respond with such aching intensity. Charlotte had never known it was even possible to feel like this. A groan of pure relief escaped as she felt the clasp of her bra released and Hawk's thumbs grazed nipples that had hardened into what felt like raw nerve endings. It was too much. And it wasn't nearly enough.

Charlotte found her fingers fumbling with the buttons of Hawk's shirt and the buckle on his belt. She had to know how far this could go. It was totally new territory for her. His touch was awakening parts of her body she hadn't realised existed. It was not so much like two bodies connecting as like finding her whole self for the first time. A being capable of experiencing a pleasure greater than anything Charlotte could have dreamed of.

No bed could have looked more inviting than the softly draped four-poster bathed in the warm glow of the old-style lamp, but it could have been an ancient mattress in the corner of a shed for all Hawk noticed. He couldn't wait a second longer. By the time he had stroked and kissed all of Charlotte's clothing aside, there was nothing more he could think to do in the way of foreplay.

So he did what he'd wanted to do for what seemed like forever. He scooped her into his arms and carried her to the nearest available surface that could provide cushioning for the kind of sexual release his body was screaming for. Looming over Charlotte on the bed, however, the desperate need abated just a little. The sight of her pale, slim body framed by the long tresses of her dark hair was so extraordinarily beautiful Hawk had to pause and catch his breath.

He had to slow down. Had to make sure this was as good for Charlotte as he knew it was going to be for him. She deserved that much consideration for the trust she was showing in him right now. He was the first in a way. The start of a new life for Charlotte. Hawk's gaze had travelled as far as Charlotte's face to find huge, dark eyes fixed on his face. Her expression mirrored precisely how he was feeling himself.

'I never knew it was possible,' she whispered, 'to want someone *this* much.'

And suddenly there was no need to slow down. No chance to try and be gentle and considerate. That could come later. Right now, Charlotte wanted this as much as he did. Just as fast. Just as hard. And just as passionately. Charlotte's cry of ecstasy only a short time later was almost matched in volume by Hawk's, and it was several minutes before either of them could speak.

'How deaf do you reckon Maggie really is?'

'I hope she's very deaf.' Charlotte caught her lower lip between her teeth as she smiled. 'Otherwise she'd know what was going on despite this cottage being the other end of the orchard.'

'We'd better be a bit quieter next time, then.'

'Next time?'

Hawk paused just long enough to kiss Charlotte. Twice. 'Are you trying to tell me that wasn't worth repeating?'

'Oh…no.' Charlotte's mouth curved in mischievous lines beneath his. 'It's just that we've got work in just a few hours. Some sleep might be a good idea.'

'I have a much better idea.' Hawk slid his hand upwards from where it rested on Charlotte's belly. He cupped the small, firm breast he had been smitten with on the first moment of discovery and the sigh he gave as he lowered his lips to her nipple was one of pure contentment.

'Mmm.' Charlotte bent her head as she pressed her lips

to the top of Hawk's head. 'You're right,' she murmured. 'This is a *much* better idea.'

A tiny part of Hawk's brain registered the fact that he was now making love to Charlotte Laing for the second time. There was a tiny alarm bell sounding to remind him that once was supposed to have been enough. Hawk silenced the alarm without a moment's hesitation.

Once could never be enough. Not when he'd found his perfect physical match. So...he wanted some more.

So what?

CHAPTER EIGHT

'SHE'S one out of the box, isn't she?'

'Sure is.'

The response was deliberately casual but Hawk cast a swift glance at the senior officer standing by his side. Lance Currie did not appear to be making any reference to an illicit liaison between colleagues, however. He was too busy watching Charlotte as she was being positioned in front of television cameras. An episode of *Crimewatch* was being filmed, having been chosen as a means of appealing for information from the public in an attempt to solve the hit-and-run case that had claimed the life of Jim Patterson two weeks ago.

'Smart, too. I know you had doubts about working with someone with Charlie's qualifications, but I wasn't wrong, was I?'

'Nope.' Hawk had no arguments with that statement. 'She's good.'

'Good enough for you to go to the trouble of persuading us to buy that incredibly expensive toy for her. Has it been used yet?'

'It was very helpful when we were assessing someone who refused to go in an ambulance after a crash last week.'

'We?' Currie raised an inquisitive eyebrow.

'Charlie's been giving me a crash course in patient assessment.' It was more difficult to sound casual now. While those out-of-hours sessions were quite serious in content, there was no need to conceal the more private communication that was adding a distinct piquancy to their working relationship these days.

'Oh?' The suggestive tone was a relief. Clearly, Currie did not suspect anything because he was enjoying this opportunity to try and get a rise out of Hawk. He gave his superior officer a very bland look.

'It's not a nice feeling not to have any idea what to do other than call for an ambulance when someone's sick or injured. I'm just making the most of an unexpected resource to gain a few new skills.'

'We have workplace first-aid courses available, you know.' Currie couldn't resist the opportunity to point out the correct station protocol for such an issue. 'I've done more than one myself.'

'And would you recognise the difference between ventricular tachycardia and ventricular fibrillation, boss? Or know what the significance is?'

The signal for quiet in the studio was the ideal way to terminate this discussion. Currie didn't have to admit he knew nothing about cardiac rhythms and Hawk no longer had to tread through any kind of verbal minefield. They both turned their gazes in the same direction the cameras were pointing.

Charlotte gave a succinct history of the incident using a map and computerised reconstruction. Then she spoke directly into the camera.

'Someone must know something,' she said persuasively. 'We know this vehicle was a red Ford Laser. An early 1980s model. We know what damage the car suffered.'

As prearranged, the camera view now changed to the table where the SCS had laid out the pieces of evidence collected from the scene. Charlotte moved to the table with a grace that belied the nervousness Hawk knew she was feeling.

'The left-hand front indicator light was smashed. The wing mirror was snapped off. It's quite possible the windscreen was damaged with what could have been a starburst pattern of cracks.'

Hawk glanced away from the live scene in front of him to where a bank of monitors displayed what was being filmed. Charlotte had refused to have her hair and make-up done for the segment, but it made no difference as far as Hawk was concerned. She looked gorgeous. He loved seeing her looking so professional in a crisp clean uniform with her hair tied back. He loved it because he knew what she looked like with no uniform on and he could imagine the slim, taut planes of her body beneath the clothing. And he knew what that magnificent hair was like when released from that long twisted rope. The way it rippled across her bare back...the way it felt when he pushed his hands into the tresses and used a length wound around a hand to bring her face close enough to kiss.

With some difficulty, Hawk concentrated on what Charlotte was saying now.

'This incident happened two weeks ago. Maybe the car hasn't been taken to a garage for repairs yet.'

Quite apart from her physical attributes, Charlotte was projecting both competence and intelligence. Currie was looking on with almost paternal pride and Hawk had the curious sensation of what could only be described as jealousy. Charlotte was *his* partner. *He* was the one who should be feeling proud of her. And he was. He just had to ensure his expression remained impassive. He didn't want Elsie, or anyone else, picking up on any undercurrents.

'Maybe this car is parked on your street,' Charlotte was saying now. 'Or in your neighbour's back yard. We want to find the driver of this vehicle and we need *your* help.' Her deliberate pause may have been due to nerves but it made the rest of her plea for assistance far more effective. 'A man died as a result of this incident and he died alone.' Large, golden-brown eyes stared into the camera with an authority that made even Lance Currie shift his feet a fraction. 'Leaving the scene of an accident without offering assistance or notifying authorities is a crime. This is a case of manslaughter and we're asking for you to help us solve it.'

The free phone line numbers available for the public to pass information on to the police were given out again and Charlotte left the studio area as the commercial break was signalled. She grimaced theatrically as she approached Hawk and Currie.

'I have *no* idea how that came across. Was it terrible?'

'It was OK,' Hawk said reassuringly.

He earned an impatient snort from Currie who then turned to Charlotte with a wide smile. 'It wasn't "OK", Charlie. It was fantastic. If we don't get a few leads after that, I'll eat my hat.'

Charlotte returned the smile but then sucked in her breath audibly. 'I *hate* television interviews,' she said. 'Next time it'll be your turn, Hawk.'

'We're far more likely to get a response from people seeing you.'

'Why? Because I'm a chick?' Charlotte's tone was challenging enough to make Currie scowl.

'When are you two going to stop bickering and realise what a tight unit you've become in the last two months? For heaven's sake, Hawk, I would have thought the issue of you working with a female officer should have been long since buried.'

The briefest glance that flashed between Hawk and Charlotte was still enough to share satisfaction that their secret was still safe. If Lance had any idea just what a tight team they had recently become, he wouldn't be congratulating them right now. He would be demanding a resignation from at least one of them.

'You guys are getting known far and wide for the speed

and thoroughness of your investigations. I'm getting requests to have you deployed to solve some of the sticky cases other areas have sitting in their files.'

'We've got quite enough work to do here,' Hawk reminded him.

'Don't I know it. It might be possible to have one of you available as a consultant if we had an extra team member, though.'

'You're thinking of expanding the team?' Charlotte didn't sound keen and Hawk could share the sentiment. They worked so well together *because* they were together. Just the two of them. Having a sizzling affair ongoing in their private lives had, if anything, made it easier to work together. The distraction of overwhelming desire had gone from work hours because they both knew it would be satisfied as soon as they reached a private space.

'It's just a thought.' Currie glanced at the team manning the phone lines. 'They look busy. Let's go and see if any useful information has come in.'

Hawk checked his watch. *Crimewatch* had only a few minutes to run, which was a relief. Very soon, he and Charlotte would be able to escape. Together. Thank goodness that plump paramedic, Laura, was still caught up in that weird babysitting situation. The fact that Charlotte was living in Laura's house gave them a retreat that was almost neutral. It enabled Hawk to keep his personal, professional and passionate lives remarkably separate, and that suited him just fine.

He had everything under control. While it was surprising that the novelty of a sexual relationship with Charlotte hadn't even begun to lose any of its appeal, despite the amount of indulgence in the last fortnight, Hawk still wasn't bothered by any resurgence of those alarm bells. This was still a temporary interlude in his life, just as all his affairs in recent years had been but, by God, he was going to make the most of it while it lasted.

'They've found the driver.'

'What driver?'

'The hit and run. He's been arrested thanks to a lead from a call to *Crimewatch*. Elsie's rapt.'

'Really? That's great!'

But Charlotte didn't look delighted for very long. Hawk raised an eyebrow. 'What's up?'

'Just a bit of a crisis at home. I need to ring Laura and make sure she's OK.'

'Why wouldn't she be?'

'She came back home just after you left last night. She was a bit upset.'

'Oh?' Hawk looked disconcerted at the news. 'Why?'

'The wheels have fallen off. The baby's mother came back. She wants the baby...and the fireman.'

'Oh. I guess Laura isn't too happy, then.'

'You don't look too happy about it either, Hawk.'

'I don't want to seem unsympathetic with your friend's plight or anything, but it will make things a bit awkward for us, won't it? When we want to...I mean, when we're not at work.'

'Maybe you'll just have to shovel up the piles of dirty socks you've got lying around at your place. Or is there something else you don't want me to see?' It hadn't bothered Charlotte that Hawk had never invited her to stay at his place. OK, maybe once hadn't been enough, but this was still just a brief fling after all. A trial period before she started a new phase of her life. So why was she feeling suddenly anxious? Would the change in arrangements be enough for Hawk to call a halt to their out-of-hours liaison?

'I don't have piles of dirty socks,' Hawk told her. 'And

people in glass houses shouldn't be chucking rocks.' He cast a pointed glance at her desk and Charlotte grinned.

She was still smiling as she reached for her pager which had sounded an urgent summons. 'Priority one to the airport,' she said. 'What's that about, do you think? A plane crash?'

'Details to follow.' Hawk snapped his pager back into its holder clipped to his belt. 'Let's go, Charlie.'

The phone call from Lance came as they were speeding towards the airport. Charlotte clicked on the speaker-phone attachment so they could both hear what was being said.

'There's a mass casualty incident just outside Hamilton,' Lance told them grimly. 'Train versus bus. We're sending some resources to back up what's coming from Auckland and I've agreed to send you two. You can catch a ride with the rescue helicopter that'll be taking off in ten minutes. You'll need to get your skates on.'

'We're nearly there.' Hawk blipped the siren as they negotiated an intersection and then turned it off so they could still hear Currie. The squad car's flashing beacons were still warning traffic of their rapid progress. 'Why us, boss?'

'Sounds messy and there's going to be huge media coverage. There's already a fuss going on about state maintenance of railway lines and some of the bus passengers include the immediate family of an All Black. Witness accounts are already contradictory. We need to get this investigation under way, pronto.'

'What's contradictory?' Charlotte queried. Interest in an MCI would be huge even without the background of a political issue or the personal involvement of a sporting hero. The more information they could get upfront, the better they would be able to handle both the investigation and any media pressure.

'Someone says the signals weren't working but another witness says a car had stopped at the crossing and the bus just ploughed into the back of it—shunted it clear, hard enough to flip it and then caught the train smack on the tail end of the bus. Half the train was derailed.'

'Good grief!' Hawk took a turn-off well before the airport terminal buildings. 'How many fatalities?'

'Ten and counting. There's still quite a few people trapped in a couple of the train carriages. A USAR team has been deployed to assist extrication. Things should be more under control by the time you get there, but do what you can. Good luck!'

'Thanks.' Hawk raised his hand to thank the airport security guard manning the gate leading directly to the area of runway designated for the rescue helicopter. 'We might need it.'

The aerial view of the incident they gained on approach was helpful in getting a perspective of the incident. It was also horrific. The snake of train carriages had a large crumpled kink that had to contain the wreckage of many human lives. The passenger bus lay on its side, the rear half-crushed. The wheels of an overturned sedan could also be seen but the evidence of death and destruction was now only part of a much larger picture.

Dozens of rescue vehicles were dotted over the scene like pieces on a vast board game. Fire appliances, ambulances, police vehicles—including a huge command centre truck. The bright colours of other rescue helicopters were nearby, and Hawk's and Charlotte's pilot was waiting for one to take off before going in to land himself.

Charlotte recognised the long igloo shape of a triage station the ambulance service had erected, and as they swooped lower she could even see the whiteboards outside that would be keeping the details of patient numbers and their status as current as possible. Hundreds of people milled about but what made the whole scene horribly real was the sight of the injured still being carried or helped towards the triage tent and, worse, a stretcher with the body completely draped bypassing the treatment area on its journey to another enclosure.

Charlotte turned to Hawk, suddenly scared of the enormity of what they were now facing. She had to shout over the noise of the rotors.

'This is *huge*.'

Hawk simply nodded, his eyes reflecting the grim reality Charlotte wasn't sure she was ready to face. Then he reached out and gripped her hand. 'We'll stay together,' he shouted back. 'We can handle this.'

And Charlotte squeezed back. Of course they could. In Hawk's company she could handle anything. She would just have to make sure they didn't get separated.

But separating them was the first thing the incident commander decided on.

'You're a paramedic, right?'

Charlotte nodded. 'But I'm here with Hawk in my capacity as a crash investigator.'

'We need you more as a paramedic right now. We've got other investigators who can work with Officer Hawkins. I want to put you with the USAR team that's dealing with trapped victims on the train. There's too many priority-one people still out there for our medics to cope with.'

So Charlotte was taken away and kitted out with medical supplies, overalls and protective gear, including goggles and a hard hat. She met the group of Urban Search and Rescue personnel that included civil defence and fire officers.

'We've just gained access to the last carriage,' the squad leader informed her. 'They've triaged and started moving the accessible patients but there's at least one person trapped under some crushed seating at one end.'

The USAR headquarters was close to the main command

area for incident management. Charlotte's attention was caught as they walked towards the train by a shower of brightly coloured cardboard tickets. Someone had tripped over a guy rope and a boxful of triage labels sent flying. Seeing something that she had used only in training exercises gave her another jolt of reality.

There were four colours of the large tickets with labelled spaces for information and a soft elastic band for attaching them to a patient's wrist or ankle. Fluorescent pink signified priority-one casualties, who were considered to have life-threatening injuries and needed the most urgent treatment and transport. Orange labels were for those who needed treatment prior to transport but whose lives would not be at risk if they weren't attended to in the shortest time frame possible. Orange labels could easily be upgraded to pink ones, however, if the patient's condition deteriorated.

Green labels were the priority-three patients with minor injuries who would be kept in a holding area and medically assessed before leaving the scene. And white labels were for the deceased. White labels could also be used for those with injuries so severe that they would require too much time and too many resources to attempt resuscitation in an MCI scenario. Charlotte was very glad she wasn't the one to have to try and make that kind of judgement today.

Near the junior ambulance officer, who was trying to collect the cards being further scattered by a stiff breeze, sat a woman with a green label on her wrist. A police officer who had been standing beside the hunched figure moved to help catch the triage labels and the woman looked up in time to catch Charlotte's stare. She felt the anguish in the eye contact like a physical blow. The green label on the woman's wrist fluttered as she scrambled to her feet.

'Are you going into the train?'

Charlotte gave a brief nod. She could see the police officer watching the woman's movements.

'My baby's in there. They can't find him. They think he might be dead but it's not true. It *can't* be true.' The woman clutched Charlotte's arm. '*Please*...bring him out to me. I'm not leaving without my baby.'

The police officer took the woman's other arm. 'Come and wait back here, Sarah. Someone's on the way to help you.'

Shaken, Charlotte continued her journey and within a short period of time she was too busy to think of the woman with the green label. Or of what Hawk might be doing. Three people still in the carriage were wearing pink labels and Charlotte found herself temporarily separated from the USAR team as she assisted first one ambulance crew and then another.

A man with broken ribs and a tension pneumothorax needed a chest needle decompression before he succumbed to a respiratory arrest. An elderly woman had lacerations to her forehead, an open fracture of her left humerus and was pale and sweaty as she told her rescuers it was her crushing, central chest pain that was her chief complaint. Charlotte administered oxygen, aspirin, GTN and morphine before they settled the woman into a Stokes basket to be carried away for urgent further assessment and treatment.

Through a carriage window, Charlotte saw Hawk walking past the command centre at one point in the company of several police photographers. Their route must have taken them past the young mother who was still sitting nearby. Despite the urgency and drama of treating the critical patients, the thought of that missing baby had remained at the back of Charlotte's mind and, even though it was probably pointless, she had found herself looking for any signs of the missing infant as she moved between patients.

The anguish the baby's mother was experiencing epitomised the feeling of this whole incident for Charlotte. She had never had a baby herself—probably never would—but she could imagine the depth of that bond and how devastating such a loss would be. And how excruciating such a wait must be, trying to hold onto a hope that one's worst fears would not be realised. Why hadn't something been done to help her yet? They must have grief counsellors or victim-support services available on scene by now. Had Hawk noticed her? Spoken to her, maybe?

'Over here, Charlie. We need a hand with a log roll.'

A teenage girl had a cervical injury. She had no sensation in her legs and pins and needles in both arms. Her breathing was abdominal and becoming laboured as her panic increased. Then Charlotte was called to the end of the carriage to rejoin the USAR team as a trapped victim was extricated from beneath mangled seating. The man was alive but his abdominal injuries were severe enough to warrant a pink tag.

It was beginning to get dark as the final victim was being freed from the carriage Charlotte was working in. Suddenly, things became chaotic.

'We need the USAR guys. Somebody heard something coming from under the carriage over there.'

Charlotte felt the same surge of adrenaline that prompted the rapid exodus of the USAR team. Had the baby been found? Alive? The bustle of movement around the man-made gap that now provided access to her carriage created enough of a new problem to distract her.

'Careful!' she warned. 'Mind that sharp edge! The IV line's—'

But her cry came too late. The IV line had been ripped clear and her patient's arm was bleeding profusely.

'Wait! Put him down,' Charlotte ordered the team of army personnel carrying the stretcher. She pulled open the pouch at her waist as she dropped to a crouch. *'Damn!'*

'Can I help?'

'Hawk!' Charlotte now had a wad of dressing pressed to the wound. 'Where did you spring from?'

'Light's getting too bad to do much more. We'll be finishing the scene maps tomorrow. What's happening here?'

'This line got ripped out. Can you put one of these gloves on and keep pressure on this while I put a new one in?'

'Why don't we get him into the triage tent?' One of the young soldiers was watching the crowed gathering around the carriage the USAR team had been deployed to.

'Because he's my patient,' Charlotte snapped. 'And he needs a patent IV urgently. This is only going to take thirty seconds.' She glanced up from pulling supplies from her pouch. Hawk's fingers of one hand were wrapped firmly around the patient's elbow. His other hand was untangling the line leading to the bag of fluids.

'Thanks, Hawk.' Charlotte was working swiftly. She tugged a tourniquet tight on the man's other arm and swabbed the inside of his elbow. 'It was hard enough getting the first line in. He's as flat as a pancake. If this doesn't work, I'll have to cannulate the jugular.'

'It'll work,' Hawk said calmly.

And it did. A doctor from the triage area arrived just as Charlotte reconnected the bag of fluid seconds later. She pumped up the pressure cuff to keep the flow as high as possible.

'Is this the guy with the abdominal trauma?'

'Yes. GCS of 7, BP unrecordable. Tachycardic. Chest's clear, though.'

'How much fluid have you got in so far?'

'Only a litre. Supply got interrupted for a minute or two here.'

'You've done well,' the doctor said. 'Thanks. We'll take over now. Looks like it's time you took a break.'

'OK.' Charlotte straightened wearily and then turned back to the carriage. 'I'll just collect the rest of my gear.'

To her surprise, Hawk followed her as she climbed through what remained of the central aisle.

'Did you find a baby in here?'

'No.' Charlotte shook her head.

'There's a woman who's been sitting out there for hours. She must have slipped through the net for the support services or something. She wants her baby.'

'I know. I've kept an eye out for it but it might not have been this carriage they were in.'

'She says it was.'

'In that case, the baby's probably dead,' Charlotte sighed. 'We haven't heard anything.'

'She needs her baby,' Hawk insisted quietly. 'Even if it *is* dead, Charlie, she needs to hold it.'

Charlotte met his gaze, astonished at the level of compassion Hawk was revealing. And, as exhausted as she was, she found the strength for renewed effort in that shared glance.

'OK. Let's look again.'

It was slow and dangerous work, methodically checking every corner of the wreckage by torchlight.

'There's no sign of it,' Charlotte said wearily, nearly an hour later.

'Babies are small.' Hawk still sounded determined. 'It *must* be here somewhere. What about that pile of luggage?'

'It's been checked. Probably more than once.'

'Let's check again.'

But Charlotte was too tired to move and to have to deal with the body of an infant would be too much now. She simply watched as Hawk pulled bag after bag from where the luggage had been hurled by the impact.

'There's a hole,' he informed her minutes later. 'Behind a suitcase, under this bent seat. More like a tunnel. Come and help me, Charlie. If we can bend the frame back a bit I can pull this case clear.'

Hawk's strength astounded Charlotte as she helped push the mangled structure of the seating a little further upright. And he was right. The back of the seat had covered a space made invisible by the wedged suitcase. She saw Hawk freeze as he stretched his arm into the space.

'I've got something.' In the peripheral light from the torch Charlotte held, she saw his face settle into horribly grim lines. 'Oh, my God,' Hawk murmured. 'It's a...it's a leg.'

And then Hawk was lying down on top of the scattered luggage, stretching into the space with both arms, and Charlotte saw the body of a tiny baby being drawn gently out. Hawk straightened, with his burden held as carefully in his arms as if it still needed his protection, and Charlotte's eyes blurred with tears.

It was in that moment that she fell in love with Owen Hawkins so deeply that she knew she would never again experience anything with such utter conviction. She loved him totally. Body and soul. She wanted to be with Hawk for the rest of her life. She wanted to hold *his* baby.

'Charlie?' Hawk's voice sounded weird and Charlotte blinked to clear the tears from her eyes.

And then she saw that the baby wasn't staring lifelessly ahead at nothing. It was staring at *her*.

'Oh, my God,' she breathed. 'Hawk...it's alive!'

The baby was not just alive. Unbelievably, the tiny boy appeared to be unscathed. The next hour was a blur for Charlotte as the baby was reunited with its mother and checked again amidst tears of joy and the kind of media excitement that such a miracle could engender, especially when highlighted against such a grim background.

Hawk was a hero but Charlotte didn't need the clamour of journalists' questions or the lights from television cameras to tell her that. She was still trying to come to terms with the stunning realisation of how she felt about him and that she was actually tempted to risk the kind of heartbreak she had vowed never to repeat. And even the joy of the baby's survival couldn't chase away the misery that temptation evoked.

Even if she *was* prepared to take that risk, she would guarantee her own failure by attempting to embrace it. The love she felt for Hawk now made her want all the things she knew he categorically *didn't* want. Marriage. Children. Permanence. The kind of commitment that kept a relationship alive long after any initial hormonal overdrive had dissipated.

The quickest way to lose what she had right now would be for Hawk to find out what she had just discovered about how she felt. He would be off like a bullet from a gun. No matter how she handled this, she was going to lose him at some point, wasn't she? It was inevitable. This was only supposed to be a fling. A game...for both of them. This was a reawakening for Charlotte that would enable her to move on to a new and complete life. They had both agreed right from the start that there were no strings and that neither of them had any intention of trying to keep things going for any longer than was prudent.

Charlotte might have just changed her mind with blinding certainty but Hawk hadn't. He had no intention of sticking around so it would make the end far less messy if he had no idea of the pain it would cause. And if she managed to keep her feelings private enough, maybe she could make it last a little longer than it might have otherwise lasted.

Maybe even long enough for Hawk to start believing in forever?

CHAPTER NINE

HAWK'S feet hit the floor within two seconds of the telephone starting to ring.

A glance at the digital bedside clock showed it was 2 a.m. but he hadn't been asleep. He reached for where his cellphone was plugged into the wall, recharging.

'Owen Hawkins.' It was probably a job and his pager just hadn't alerted him for some reason. He *hoped* it was a job. He already knew it was going to be a long and lonely night without Charlotte. This was the first night they'd had completely apart in more than two weeks. Last night, when they had been billeted close to the scene of the mass casualty incident, hadn't counted. That had been work.

'Hawk! How *are* you, buddy?'

'Cam!' Hawk was shaking his head around his grin. 'Have you any idea what time it is here?'

'Nope. Couldn't be bothered trying to work it out. You haven't answered my emails for two days, mate. Are you in love or something?'

'As if!' Hawk turned his pillow sideways to use as a cushion as he flopped back onto his bed. 'I've been out of town for two days. Big MCI up north.'

'Yeah? What was it?'

'Train versus bus versus car. Messy.'

'Fatalities?'

'Fifteen at the last count. There's a few listed as critically ill so it might climb. I'm surprised you haven't heard about it on your side of the world.'

'I've been too busy to take much notice of anything. I've got something exciting to tell you, buddy.'

156

'Oh, no.' Hawk groaned. 'Cassie's having twins, right?'

'Hell, I hope not. One will be quite enough to start with, thanks. No, Cassie's decided she wants to emigrate. Guess where we're going to live?'

Hawk's grin was back again. 'You're coming home?'

'Too right we are.'

'But that's fantastic!' This was just the news Hawk needed to hear. The repercussions of the traumatic job over the last two days were proving very difficult to shake off. Hawk felt as if something fundamental in his world had changed but he couldn't put his finger on it and it was difficult to try and get things back into proper perspective. The prospect of regaining the old stability of being with Cam was enormously appealing. 'When? Soon, I hope.'

'No, not for a while. We want the kid to be born over here so we can give it an American passport.'

'But that's months away. Couldn't you come back and just pop over for the birth?'

Cam laughed. 'Wouldn't want to, mate. I'm having a blast meeting all Cassie's relatives and seeing a bit of the country on my days off. We're going to take an extended tour for a honeymoon but right now we're up to our necks in wedding preparations. Which was the other reason I rang. Listen, Hawk... I want you to change your mind about coming over to be my best man.'

'I thought one of Cassie's brothers was going to fill the breach.'

'It wouldn't be the same.' Cam sounded serious now. 'This is a big deal, mate, and I don't want to sound soppy or anything but I'm not sure I want to do it unless you're there with me.'

Now it was Hawk's turn to laugh. 'So don't do it! Come home and get back to work where you belong.' The words came easily enough. It had been something of a standard exchange for at least a month after Cam had left but, for the first time, something didn't feel right as he said them. He did miss Cam—of course he did. But saying so suddenly seemed like disloyalty to Charlotte. And if Cam came back, where would Charlotte go?

'That's another thing. I spoke to Elsie a couple of days ago. Did he tell you?'

'No, but we've all been pretty distracted by the MCI and it was pretty late when we got back tonight. It was some scene map to do and there were a hundred and fifty people that had to be interviewed for potential witness statements.'

'Phew! How come you got involved if it was up north?'

Hawk couldn't tell him of the reputation he and Charlotte were gaining as being such a good team. 'They needed all the help they could get.'

'Was it gruesome?'

'I'm glad it's over.' Hawk didn't want to dwell on that any more. 'So, what did Elsie have to say, anyway?'

The silence was tiny but significant. 'He's not keen on extending my leave. If I want my job back I need to make a decision, and if I decide to keep the job I'll need to front up pretty soon.'

'You mean you're thinking of *not* keeping it?' It should have been a disappointing notion. Why did it allow a tiny glow of warmth somewhere in that hollow feeling that had been hanging around in his gut for the last twenty-four hours or so? Because it meant that he'd be able to keep working with Charlotte maybe? But if he kept working with her, he'd have to stop sleeping with her. Sooner or later someone was going to twig to the fact that they were lovers. Maybe not lovers exactly, but they were both active participants in a physical game they seemed to gain equal pleasure from playing.

'I'm not sure,' Cam told him. 'It's funny, but my career doesn't seem all that important just now. I mean, I love the work and I really miss having you for a partner, mate, but

I'm not going to let my career wreck what Cassie and I have together. There *is* more to life than work, you know.'

'There is?' Hawk's attempt at humour sounded flat even to his own ears. He might have made the quip in all sincerity except that it had been a recurring thought of his own during the sleepless hours he had already spent lying on his bed tonight.

The uncharacteristic reassessment of values was obviously a reaction to the incident he'd just been involved in. He had learnt long ago that there were no guarantees in life as far as relationships with women were concerned, but the whole, horrible aftermath of the train crash had reminded him that there were no guarantees in life, full stop. What *did* really matter when life could be snuffed out with such devastating unexpectedness? A career? Hardly. Friends? Definitely.

'Of course there is.' He answered his own quip before Cam had a chance to. 'I'll have a word with Elsie on your behalf if you like, mate. I'm sure we could work something out. Charlie would probably be keen to stay on and the boss *was* making noises about needing an extra team member before long anyway, with the workload we've got. Maybe we could swing us all working together. You'd like Charlie, Cam. She's great to work with once you get used to her.'

'Hmm. Elsie said something about that as well. I almost got the impression he was looking for an excuse to employ her on a permanent basis. Hey, you haven't started *preferring* to work with a chick, have you?'

Hawk's laughter was genuine for a moment. 'There's no comparison, mate.'

Cam must have sensed something in the way Hawk's laughter had faded a little abruptly. Or in the short silence that followed.

'You're not *sleeping* with her, are you, mate?'

Hawk made no response and Cam's astonished oath filled the silence.

'Does Elsie know?'

'No.'

'You'd better keep it quiet, then. Otherwise she won't be allowed to hang around long enough to keep my seat warm. You know the rules. And you know what a stickler Elsie is for following them. Look at the way he's reacting to the suggestion I extend my leave.'

'Yeah. I know.'

'Is it worth the risk?'

Hawk's attempt at light laughter stuck in his throat somewhere. 'Yeah…it's worth it.'

'Oh, boy. This is serious.'

'Of course it isn't. It's just a fling.'

'Does *she* know that?'

'Of course she does. That's the way she wants it as well. She's still hung up on a fiancé that got killed just before their wedding.'

'How long has this been going on?'

'Only a few weeks.'

'And you're not bored yet?'

'Are you kidding? She's…she's, I don't know…different.'

'Doesn't sound like you, mate.' Cam sounded as though he was shaking his head. 'Could be the old love bug biting.'

The attempt at a disparaging chuckle was successful this time. 'No way.' And he meant it. Didn't he? Except… except he couldn't stop thinking about the moment he'd found that baby. When they'd both been expecting the confirmation of another tragedy. Hawk had known how terrible that would be as he'd pulled the baby out and he'd also known with absolute conviction that when it was over he would need the wordless comfort that only Charlotte's touch could give him.

Instead, it had become a moment of pure joy. A joy that was even more overwhelming because it was being shared…with Charlotte. Was this what love really was? That feeling of desperate need and knowing that comfort would be available? Or that feeling of shared joy? Knowing that similar moments could occur in the future and wanting to share them with that same person?

A devil's advocate surfaced from nowhere to remind Hawk of his long-held stance. 'Me and serious is an oxymoron when it comes to women, Cam. You should know that better than anyone.'

'Yeah, but things change,' Cam said thoughtfully. 'Like I used to share your belief that babies were alien monsters of some kind. I hate to admit this but I actually *enjoyed* choosing bootees and stuff at the baby shop yesterday.' Hawk heard Cam give what sounded like a contented sigh. 'You've got no idea how cute some of that stuff is.'

Hawk was silent again. Sarah's baby had been wearing bootees with some kind of animal ears and whiskers on them. They had been the first thing he'd touched as he'd reached into that void beneath the seat.

'Have you ever even held a baby, Hawk?'

'Actually, I did. Yesterday.'

'No kidding?'

'Yeah. You won't believe this story, Cam.' And Hawk talked on, telling his friend about the long search and the baby's miraculous survival.

'You need me around, mate,' Cam said finally. 'Sounds like a celebratory beer or two is in order here.'

'Yeah.' But Hawk's agreement was a shade half-hearted. Reliving that moment of finding the baby alive had made him remember the way Charlotte's eyes had shone with happy tears. The way her smile had started so slowly and then grown…and grown, until they'd both been laughing and crying at the same time. What he really needed was

Charlotte's company. He wanted to see her smile again. To hear her laugh. Why had it seemed so awkward to suggest that she come back to his place when they'd returned to Wellington that evening? And why had she seemed so keen to get home?

'What I probably need is some sleep,' Hawk told Cam. 'It's nearly 3 a.m. here, mate.'

'Good grief. I hate to think what my phone bill's going to be like. All I really intended to do was persuade you to come to our wedding. Cassie thinks you hate her.'

'I don't,' Hawk said firmly. 'Look, leave it with me, Cam. My batteries are getting low here so I'd better go. I'll have a look at the rosters and see whether it's even possible for me to get away for a few days. I'll talk to Elsie. I'll email you.'

Hawk plugged his phone back into the charger. He didn't hate Cassie. He didn't even feel jealous of the time and commitment she had won with Cam any more. He did feel jealous, though. He recognised the hard knot that had formed in that weird hollow place at some point in his conversation with Cam. He could even recognise *why* he felt jealous. Cam had something in his life that Hawk didn't have. Permanence. Marriage and…and kids on the way.

Hawk wanted it, too. With Charlotte. He wanted it all and he wanted it forever. The realisation was unnerving and Hawk had absolutely no idea what he could do about it. He only knew what he couldn't do and that was to say anything to Charlotte. She'd be off like a scalded cat if he even hinted at wanting all the things he knew she *didn't* want.

Spending one night totally apart from her was bad enough. The thought of spending the rest of his life alone was unbearable. It wasn't just a question of what he needed or wanted himself. He wanted to give the same back. To be as important to Charlotte as she had become to him. And with that realisation came another truth. *This* was the basis of true love.

So it had finally happened. Hawk knew what it was like to be totally in love with someone. Why the hell did it have to happen with totally the wrong woman?

Charlotte's paramedic kit was heavy enough to make her wish she had taken the lift instead of struggling up all the stairs from the basement garage. She paused for a moment, not wanting Hawk to see she was out of breath as she arrived back in the office. He should have gone and got the kit himself. After all, it was for his benefit that they were having another one of their private training sessions tonight.

She hadn't been averse to the idea, though, had she? It felt a lot longer than four days since that MCI now and they hadn't been together out of work hours. The amount of work generated by the incident had been phenomenal. Hawk had had to travel to Hamilton for a two-day session with all the other investigators involved so that a report could be finalised. Charlotte had been left holding the fort, and by the time Hawk had returned yesterday she had so much paperwork to catch up on there was no way she could avoid working late. And alone.

She knew it wasn't being used as a convenient backing-out point by Hawk, however. The smouldering look he'd given her when he'd arrived at work that morning had let her know he was missing their private time together just as much as she was. Sexual tension had been building all day. A look here, a casual touch in passing there. The suggestion that it was time Hawk continued his training as a paramedic's assistant was surely just a prelude to a more intimate occasion, and Laura was working a night shift so they could have the house to themselves if they wanted it.

It was perfect. Or it would have been if Hawk had offered to go and fetch the kit from the squad car himself. But Lance had popped in on his way out of the department and the two men had looked set for a chat that hadn't included Charlotte. As she paused to catch her breath and rest her arm muscles, she realised why she hadn't passed her boss on the stairs as she'd expected. He was still talking to Hawk, and in the quiet of the otherwise deserted department his voice carried with absolute clarity.

'It puts me in a bit of a dilemma, Hawk. Cam wants his job back but he wants it on his terms. It might be a year before he's back on deck full-time.'

Charlotte shamelessly stood still and eavesdropped. A year? But that was great.

'Regulations about leaving a permanent position unfilled are quite clear,' Lance was saying now. 'The three months' leave is rapidly running out. If Cam's not prepared to get back here then the position will have to be advertised. Cam could apply for it like anyone else and if he was successful then he *would* be in a position to negotiate a starting date.'

'Does he know that?'

'Well, I told him so in no uncertain terms. I also told him that Charlotte Laing would probably apply for the position and that she'd be a strong contender. Very strong.' Currie's voice lowered a little and Charlotte found herself straining to hear his next words. 'I like the way you two work together, Hawk. I'm really impressed with the way the department is heading and I want to keep her on board.'

'What about expanding the team? We could use extra manpower, you've said so yourself.'

'You, Cam and Charlie? Hmm. Interesting idea but it's not on the table at this point in time and I *have* to get something done about this vacancy.'

'What are you going to do?'

'I'm going to throw the ball into your court, Hawk, that's what I'm going to do. You get to choose. If you want to continue working with Charlie, just say so and I'll get the application process under way. If you want Cam as a partner again, I'll do what I can to get his leave extended.'

'That puts me in a difficult position.'

'Nobody will know that except you and me, Hawk. Put it in writing, mark it confidential and leave it on my desk.' Currie's voice got louder. He was probably moving towards the office door. Hastily Charlotte picked up her kit, moved backwards a few steps and then started forward again, making herself sound slightly out of breath as she neared the office door.

Lance was just emerging as she got there. 'Hi, Charlie. Don't work too late, now, will you?' He poked his head back into the office. 'Tomorrow would be good, Hawk, if you can manage it.'

'Sure.' Hawk made it sound as though Lance wanted nothing more than a photocopy of some report but Charlotte knew better. She eyed Hawk with more than a little uncertainty.

'Are you sure you want to spend any time on this? We can leave it for another day if you've got more important things to do.'

Hawk shook his head. 'I've been looking forward to this. Show me your wares, woman.'

The quirk of an eyebrow suggested that he was interested in far more than what her paramedic kit contained. Charlotte grinned, placed the kit on Hawk's desk and opened it before pulling herself up to sit alongside the large container. 'OK, what can you see that you recognise?'

'I can see that my desk is a lot tidier than yours. You'd never find enough empty space on yours to fit a kit and a bottom—however attractively small that bottom might be.'

'Pay attention here, Officer Hawkins,' Charlotte said sternly. 'I thought you wanted to do this.'

'Maybe there's something else I want more now.'

'OK.' Charlotte started to close the kit but Hawk's hand caught her wrist.

'No. You've gone to all the trouble of fetching this so I want to learn something.' His thumb rubbed the inside of Charlotte's wrist, sending shivers of delight into parts of her anatomy that couldn't possibly have any connection to her wrist. 'Let's just keep it short and simple. I'm not sure how long I'll be able to concentrate.'

Probably longer than she would. Charlotte found it difficult to remember what she'd been saying.

Hawk grinned at her expression, then let go of her wrist and eyed the kit.

'Right. I recognise lots of stuff here. A blood-pressure cuff, a bag mask set-up, lots of different drugs and all sorts of IV gear.'

'Say I have a patient with hypovolaemic shock. I need to get fluids running but I'm busy with other assessments so I ask you to set up the gear for an IV. Pull out everything you're going to need and set it up for me.'

'What gauge cannula do you want, sir?'

'She's in shock. We'll need a 14.' Charlotte bit back her smile. Hawk might be adding a bit of humour here but she knew how intense his concentration would be despite any distractions. He would remember everything he'd learn as well. He'd already shown how seriously he took these training sessions and they had progressed well beyond him being able to perform effective cardiopulmonary resuscitation.

Hawk's eyes gleamed at her attempt to hide her amusement and then Charlotte had to smile. How could she have ever thought of him as aloof? Or fierce, as Laura had been convinced he was. Sure, Hawk didn't smile or laugh as often as Jamie had, but that only made his expressions of pleasure more meaningful. And, yes, he was intense and that could come across as being intimidating but Charlotte appreciated it now.

She watched his deft movements as he chose items from her kit. A cannula package of the correct gauge, a tourniquet, an alcohol wipe, a luer plug, tape and a dressing.

A lot of people probably made the mistake of judging Hawk on initial impressions, which would explain why he didn't have the popularity Jamie had enjoyed. But the friends Hawk did have were close and very loyal and Charlotte could understand why. With Jamie she might have been special but she had still been one of a crowd. With Hawk, Charlotte could feel she was the only one that mattered.

Hawk reached for a 5 ml syringe and some saline to draw up a flush. He glanced up for a second, gained an approving nod from Charlotte and winked at her before turning back to his task. Just the kind of secret communication they enjoyed while keeping their at-work interaction respectable enough not to raise anyone's suspicions. How much of the feeling of being so special came from having to keep their relationship a secret?

Not all of it, Charlotte was sure of that. Amazing to think she had been so angry when Hawk had expressed disapproval that Jamie had spent the night before their wedding out with his mates. Now that she knew what it was like to be the sole focus of a man's attention, Charlotte could share that disapproval. If she'd been special enough to marry, why hadn't she been the one he'd wanted to be with that night?

Charlotte brushed the thought aside. Dwelling on the past was pointless. Comparing Hawk and Jamie was also pointless. Memories of Jamie were where they should be now. Tucked away in a place that would not allow them to cause any more pain. At least, not enough pain to hold her back from getting as much joy as she could from her future.

'That's great, Hawk,' she congratulated him. 'Now find the GTN spray.'

Hawk had to pull open the tray containing the drugs to find the small cannister. Charlotte's phone beeped to signal a text and Hawk glanced up again. 'That wasn't your pager, was it?'

'No—just a text from Laura. She's on night shift and wants me to bring in her washing later if it's dry.' It was the first time Laura had been on night shift since she'd moved back home. The first opportunity Charlotte and Hawk had had in what seemed like a very long time to really be together again.

'Night shift,' Hawk echoed softly. 'What time does she get home?'

'She finishes at 7 a.m.' It was almost 7 p.m. now. If they left soon they could have twelve hours together. The way Charlotte was feeling right now she wasn't sure it would be long enough to satisfy her. On the other hand, she'd had a lot of time to think about Hawk over the last few days and nothing had shaken her discovery of how deeply she felt. Would it be possible to make love and not reveal too much? She felt almost as nervous as the first time she had contemplated going to bed with him.

'Has she sorted out the problems with that guy she's keen on?'

'Not yet.' Charlotte sighed, pleased to turn her thoughts, albeit temporarily, to someone else's romantic problems. 'Poor Laura. She's got her heart set on getting married and having a family. It's even more important to her than her career.'

'Amazing that you two are such good friends when you want such different things out of life.'

Charlotte stared at her phone as she clipped it back to her belt. She needed to be very careful what she said here, if she didn't want to reveal anything that might scare Hawk off. She managed a light laugh. 'Just as well we both think along the same lines, isn't it, Hawk? You want marriage and kids just as much as I do.'

'Like a hole in the head, huh?' Hawk's voice sounded odd and Charlotte risked a quick glance. Had he sensed any insincerity in what had been intended as a reassuring statement?

'Absolutely.' Her gaze flicked to the spray he was holding. 'Tell me about GTN.'

'Glyceryl trinitrate,' Hawk said promptly. He seemed as eager as Charlotte was to change the subject. 'It's a rapid-acting vasodilator, which is particularly effective in relieving the symptoms of coronary artery spasm or angina.'

'Cool. How does it do that?'

'Vasodilation increases coronary blood supply. Dilation of the venous system decreases pre-load or filling pressure which decreases the workload of the heart, and dilation of the arterial system decreases aortic pressure which reduces after-load. Reducing the workload of the heart reduces the need for oxygen and it's getting more anyway because of the dilated coronary vessels.'

'OK, I'm impressed. You're picking up this stuff so fast you'll know just as much as I do soon.'

'It's fun.' Hawk's gaze held what seemed like a serious question. 'Do you miss it, Charlie? Being a full-time paramedic?'

'Not really. I've got the best of both worlds with this job. I love the crash investigation side just as much as working with patients.'

'So you wouldn't go back to being a paramedic, then, if…if things didn't work out here long term?'

Charlotte shrugged. 'I suppose I'll have to consider that if Cam decides to come back.' She didn't want Hawk to know she'd overheard his conversation with Lance Currie. And she couldn't let him know how much she wanted to continue working with *him*. 'I don't really want to move away from Wellington.'

'You mean you want to live here permanently?'

'Nothing has to be permanent.' Charlotte smiled to show Hawk that she could handle the inevitable changes that occurred in life. She wasn't expecting him to commit to anything long term and she wasn't going to hold any hard feelings when he decided it was time to call off their affair. 'But for the foreseeable future it seems like a good place to be. I've never had a place to really call home. Maybe it's time I put down a few roots.'

'Even if they're going to need pulling up sometime?'

Charlotte shrugged. 'If plants never put down roots they would never get to grow much, would they? Sure, they might wilt a bit when they get transplanted but they're bigger than they were and they recover. Except for hundred-year-old trees.' Charlotte grinned. 'But by the time I reach my century I expect the only moving I'll want to do is in my rocking chair.'

'I can't imagine you as an old crone.' Hawk had a curiously thoughtful expression. Or was it more like disguised horror?

'Don't worry, Hawk.' Charlotte said soothingly. 'It won't be your problem.'

To her surprise, Hawk didn't appear at all soothed. 'So it wouldn't bother you to change jobs, then? You could just wilt a bit and then sprout out in new directions?'

'Of course it would bother me. My career has been my life for a long time now and I would rather be doing this than any other job. I'm good at it,' she added a little defensively. 'And Elsie told me only last week that I'd have a good chance of being successful if the job gets advertised.'

Hawk wasn't meeting her gaze. Was he worried that she *might* win the position over Cam? He'd resent her if she did. 'But then again,' she added, 'you've helped me realise that there is more to life than just work, Hawk, and I'll always be grateful for that.'

He was looking at her now but Charlotte couldn't read the expression in those dark eyes with any accuracy. If it wasn't so unbelievable she might think he was fearful that she was about to tell him their affair was over. More likely, he was afraid she was about to say that he was more important to her than her career.

'It's getting late,' she observed. 'Shall we pack up here and go and find something to eat?'

'Sure. I'm pretty hungry.' Hawk's expression advertised relief now. Probably because the potentially heavy conversation was over. Then it started revealing something else. Something Charlotte hadn't seen with such strength since before the disruption of that mass casualty incident.

Desire. Hot and strong and absolutely compelling. She snapped the latches shut on her kit. 'Just as well Laura's on night shift,' she murmured.

'I was thinking it was time you came home with me for a change.'

Charlotte swallowed. The invitation may have sounded casual but it had been charged with significance. Hawk merely shrugged at her raised eyebrows.

'I'd hate to have picked up all those piles of dirty socks for nothing.'

'Sure.' Charlotte eased herself down from where she was still sitting on Hawk's desk and lifted her kit clear. 'I'm ready,' she told him. 'Shall we go?'

'Just give me a couple of minutes,' Hawk said. 'There's something Elsie wants on his desk by tomorrow so I'd better get it done.'

'Can I help?'

'No…it's nothing much. Just an opinion on something,

really.' Hawk's body language made his verbal attempt to make the task seem unimportant a complete failure.

Ten minutes later Charlotte had to grit her teeth when Hawk dropped the sealed envelope on Lance Currie's desk as they passed the senior sergeant's office on their way out of the department. She knew what was in that envelope. The choice. Given the pointed conversation about how she felt about the job, she could be certain that Hawk was asking to have Cam back as his partner. It was unavoidable. Charlotte couldn't take the job anyway. Imagine trying to work with Hawk once their affair was over? It would be totally impossible. Lance was right to make sure his officers stuck to the rules.

Did what was in the letter also explain the significant invitation to go home to Hawk's house tonight? Was the writing on the wall for their time together, so it didn't matter if he let her that little bit further into his life? She should pull away. If this was potentially their last night together, why was she allowing Hawk to hold her hand and lead her forward?

Because there was no way she could resist. Any thought of self-preservation or even pride died at the caress of Hawk's thumb moving over her fingers. She held onto his hand just as she was going to hold onto every moment she could have with this man she loved.

Even one extra night, especially in his own home…his own bed, would provide memories. And those she *would* be able to hold onto for the rest of her life.

CHAPTER TEN

Two sealed envelopes lay on Lance Currie's desk the following morning.

Both were marked 'Confidential'. He opened and read first one and then the other letter. He read them again. He leaned back in his chair, closed his eyes and let out a long, loud and very exasperated sigh. Then his eyes snapped open again and he snatched up his telephone.

'Get hold of Hawkins and Laing,' he snapped at the operator. 'I want them both in my office, pronto!'

'They're out on a job, sir. They got despatched ten minutes ago to a fatality on Birches Road.'

Currie made another exasperated sound. 'Page them, then,' he ordered. 'And the minute they set foot back in this building they can march themselves straight up here.'

He shook his head as he shoved the letters to one side of his desk. The job involving the Serious Crash Squad had better not be too time-consuming. This needed sorting out.

Just what the *hell* did those two think they were playing at here?

'This shouldn't take too long.'

'No.' Charlotte gazed at the scene of devastation in front of them. An ordinary little car that no longer looked at all ordinary. Instead, it looked as though it had been pierced by a giant set of spreaders, ripped open and then stretched apart on the driver's side until it had bent back and virtually snapped in half.

Beside the widened space that should have been the driver's compartment, a crumpled figure lay face down on

173

the grass verge. An ambulance crew were packing up their gear and their expressions left no doubt that there was nothing they could do to help this victim.

Maybe it wouldn't be so bad walking away from this job. At least as a paramedic the fatalities Charlotte had to deal with would not be an intrinsic component of every callout. She would be helping more people who were sick rather than severely injured and the sight of mangled vehicles would only represent a tiny percentage of her workload.

She was feeling slightly sick herself right now, having read the message on her pager. She could guess why Lance was demanding an immediate interview when they returned from this job. Hawk had read the message as well but, instead of making some kind of joke about the trouble Charlotte might have got them into, he had simply turned and walked closer to the wreck on the side of the road.

Charlotte followed more slowly. She was beginning to think that dropping that envelope on Currie's desk that morning had not been the right thing to do after all. The decision to do so had been impulsively made as she'd driven home from Hawk's house early that morning to find the clean uniform items she needed for the day. The glow that the aftermath of a night's love-making with Hawk had left her with had also prompted a wry smile as Charlotte remembered telling him with such conviction that there was no chance of anything coming from their mutual attraction because there was no way she would risk losing her job. Right then she'd have given her job up in a flash if it could have meant keeping what she had found with him, and that was what had made her intended course of action seem so obvious.

She would resign from her job.

'You can see the imprint of the power pole on the middle of the driver's door.' Hawk didn't need to point out the obvious to Charlotte but she merely nodded. 'Looks like the car's rotated and then hit the pole again just above the B pillar.'

'The pole's shattered at the base.' Charlotte took a photograph of the unstable base of the concrete pole. 'Lucky we haven't got any wires down, isn't it?' The question was as redundant as Hawk's observation but a question of some sort seemed like the best way of catching his eye.

'The road's still icy.' Finding something to look at rather than Charlotte seemed deliberate. 'And it doesn't look as though it's had any grit put down recently.'

'Nobody expects frosts at this time of year. This would have melted well before now if that hedge wasn't shading the road.'

'Road surface is good.' Hawk scuffed at the chip seal with the toe of his boot. 'If she hadn't either braked or accelerated there shouldn't have been any reason to skid.'

'Maybe she was speeding.'

'Speedo's locked at eighty.' Hawk was turning away again as Charlotte glanced up from the camera's viewfinder. 'I would have thought you'd have spotted that.'

Charlotte ignored the criticism. She probably would have spotted it if she hadn't been preoccupied by Hawk's odd mood. He'd been shut up like a clam ever since she'd arrived at work that morning. Sure, the callout had come within minutes of her arrival but their interchanges since had been more strictly professional than their game of pretence called for. And there was no reason to have kept it up in the privacy of the squad car. But maybe his avoidance of anything as personal as a touch or eye contact was not so odd at all. *His* letter had still been on Lance Currie's desk when Charlotte had delivered hers. Was Hawk thinking about how she was going to react when she learned of its contents?

With a sigh, Charlotte turned back to taking photographs

of the car. The floor pan had been ripped apart and the bottom of the A pillar torn away from the front of the vehicle. No wonder it looked far longer than normal. Hawk was taking notes as he spoke to the ambulance officers and other police still on scene, and he was being shown the victim's driver's licence and other items from the young woman's handbag.

It had to have been the right thing to do. Things certainly couldn't carry on the way they were. If she and Hawk continued working together *and* continued their affair, it would be discovered eventually and cause trouble that might have repercussions on Hawk that could only lead to resentment. If they continued working together and their affair ended, Charlotte would find it unbearable to be so close to the man she loved but couldn't be with.

The necessity to force Hawk to choose between her and Cam as a permanent partner would be removed by her resignation. It would, in fact, be giving him a far more important choice as far as Charlotte was concerned. If she stayed in the same city but in a different job then there would be no professional restraints on their relationship. Hawk could choose whether he wanted it to continue or not, and if he did choose to continue then Charlotte would know that there was some hope for the future.

But was she taking a gamble she couldn't afford to lose? It was possible she could continue working with Hawk and that their affair could remain secret and continue long enough to develop into something strong enough to overcome Hawk's prejudices. For him to share her belief that what they had was special enough to last a lifetime. Was she throwing that opportunity away needlessly? Would he find out what she had done or would Lance simply take her resignation and Hawk's request to have Cam as his partner as a neat solution to his current personnel problem? The hiccup would be in finding someone to fill in an extension to Cam's leave of absence. Charlotte had requested that her resignation become effective immediately.

Well, they could sort that out themselves. Hawk would probably be as relieved as Elsie to have her gone. His withdrawn professionalism this morning was really starting to get on Charlotte's nerves in a big way. Good grief, all she wanted was a smile or even a look that didn't make her feel like her presence was as welcome as rain on a picnic. Charlotte's inaudible mutter matched the scowl on her face as she marched down the road to take a photograph of the permanent advisory sign warning that the road would be slippery in frosty conditions.

Hawk watched Charlotte's purposeful journey towards the road sign. It was a relief to allow his eyes to rest on her for more than a second or two. He wasn't used to feeling nervous and he didn't like it. Charlotte was behaving oddly as well. Had she picked up on his state of mind? Given their love-making of the night before, it seemed inevitable that he had revealed more about how he felt than he'd intended.

Maybe she *had* guessed and was looking for a way out. That would explain the rather intense stares he had been deliberately avoiding all morning. If that was the case then he'd made a big mistake in that letter he'd left on Elsie's desk yesterday evening. He had taken a huge gamble and Hawk had a horrible feeling that he wasn't going to win.

The sense of foreboding congealed into a heaviness that was far deeper than disappointment, but Hawk wasn't going to try and analyse the unpleasant sensation. There would be more than enough time for that later. Right now they had a job to do. And when they had finished here they would have to go and face the music in their senior sergeant's office. This was possibly degenerating into the worst day in Hawk's life. He could feel his face settle into determined and probably sour lines as he strode towards the squad car to collect the equipment he needed to measure the surface friction of the road.

The atmosphere deteriorated further on the trip back to the city.

'How high do you reckon that hedge was?' It was Charlotte who had broken a rather uncomfortable silence.

'A good three metres.'

'It shades half the road. It's a death trap.'

'That's why the skid warning sign for frost is on the road.'

'There are regulations about growing hedges that shade the road. This one needs cutting down.'

'The limits only apply to plantings made after the regulations came into force.'

'So you're saying the farmer should be allowed to keep it?'

'I'm saying he can't be forced to cut it down. We can make a recommendation but that's as far as it goes.'

'So it's all right to keep something that's killed somebody, then.'

Hawk pressed his lips together to prevent an answering snap. Why was Charlotte being like this? They'd just spent a night together and as far as he was concerned it had been the most amazing night of his life. He had come *that* close to confessing how he felt as he'd held Charlotte in his arms after their love-making. Asking her to *marry* him, for God's sake. Now she was treating him as though he'd done something unforgivable.

He knew what it was. Emotional manipulation. He could feel the suck of those tentacles. Charlotte was upset about something. She wanted something from him that he wasn't providing and she was dealing with it precisely like every woman he had ever known.

He'd asked what was wrong the minute she'd arrived at

work and had given him that strange look. And she'd said, 'Nothing.' He knew he was supposed to put the effort into finding what the 'nothing' was and he would have done so if that call hadn't come in. Maybe it was just as well he had lost the inclination as they'd responded to the job.

It was precisely the kind of wake-up call Hawk had been expecting all along. He'd been here before. This was the time to cut and run. Before those tentacles got enough of a hold to make him actually respond to the manipulation and try and winkle out the cause of the upset and put it right. Jump through the emotional hoops, in other words. Well, he wasn't playing this game. Hawk's lips felt glued together by now and they could just stay like that.

Lance Currie eyed the two stony-faced officers sitting on the other side of his desk and sighed inwardly. He picked up the two letters and looked pointedly at Hawk before transferring the look to Charlotte.

'Is somebody going to tell me what's going on, here? What kind of game you both seem to be playing?'

Hawk said nothing and Charlotte licked her lips nervously. Currie didn't look as though he had been presented with a solution to any staffing problems. He looked... furious. The silence ticked on until it was unbearable.

'I...uh...I don't feel I can work with Hawk any longer.'

'Why the hell not?' The tone of Currie's voice was matched by the expression that replaced the astonishment on Hawk's face. Now they were both angry.

Because I'm in love with him, Charlotte shouted silently. And he doesn't feel the same way. She shut her eyes for a split second to banish the words echoing in her head.

'I...I overheard the conversation you were having with Hawk yesterday.' Charlotte stared at the blade of grass stuck to the side of her boot. She would have to clean the remnants of that verge off her footwear as soon as this was over.

'What conversation?' Lance Currie's eyes narrowed. 'Be a bit more specific, can't you, Officer Laing?'

'You were discussing whether or not to extend Cam's leave of absence.' Charlotte spoke more confidently now. This was a good tack to take. It made sense *and* it was safe. 'You asked Hawk to let you know his preference for a permanent partner. I know how much he's missed working with Cam and I don't want to try and take his place.' She warmed to her explanation. 'Being seen as the reason such a tight team was broken up would only cause resentment that would not be conducive to a productive work environment.'

'What?' Hawk spoke for the first time since they'd entered the senior sergeant's office. 'What the hell *is* this rubbish, Charlie?'

'It's not rubbish,' Charlotte retorted. 'You resented me the minute I walked in here. No…you started resenting me even *before* I set foot on your patch, according to what Laura said.'

'Who's Laura?'

Charlotte ignored Lance's query. 'You didn't want someone replacing your best mate. You didn't want a woman and you didn't want someone who was trying to do two jobs at once who would waste time *fluffing* around on scene.'

'For heaven's sake, Charlie, you're spouting ancient history here. Sure, I had my doubts about you at first…'

Currie was looking even more bemused now. 'Fluffing?' he echoed belatedly.

'You proved me wrong and you know that as well as I do.' Hawk's stare was accusatory. 'Why do you think I've been getting you to give me all those training sessions on paramedic stuff? I admire what you're capable of. I respect the fact that you're more qualified than I am in that area. I think the added dimension you bring to this unit has made it unique.'

'So do I.' Currie nodded emphatically. Then he shook his head. *'Fluffing?'*

Hawk was shaking his head. 'I don't understand this,' he growled. 'If I had to make a choice between working with you and *anyone* else, you'd win hands down, Charlie. And you go and resign without even talking to me about it?' His face showed genuine pain now and Lance blinked. There was more going on here than he'd realised.

'So you want to go on working with Charlie, then?' he asked.

'Of course I do.'

'So why is your letter of resignation here along with hers?'

Charlotte gasped. Hawk's letter had been one of resignation? 'You said you'd worked too hard to get where you are—that you weren't going to do anything that might cost you your job.'

'I was agreeing with you, if you remember. *You* said it first.'

'Well, that makes sense,' Currie sighed. 'Neither of you intend to lose your jobs so you both hand in your resignation on the same day.'

'I'm allowed to change my mind,' Charlotte snapped. 'I'm a woman, remember?'

'That's not something I'm going to forget in a hurry, unfortunately.'

'Unfortunately?' Currie's bushy eyebrows came together in a deep scowl. 'You said that the problem of Charlie being female was ancient history, Hawk.'

'This has nothing to do with work, Elsie.'

'Aha!' Currie's face settled into exasperated lines. 'I *knew* it.' Then he frowned again. *'Elsie?'*

Another silence was adding to the tense atmosphere in the office. Lance rested his elbows on his desk and pressed the fingertips of both hands together. 'Personal relationships between colleagues in the same department that interfere with the running of that department are specifically mentioned in contracts as not being permissible.' He drummed his fingertips together irritably. 'I'd say having the staff of an entire department resign *en masse* could be considered interference in the running of that department, wouldn't you?'

Hawk shrugged. 'That's precisely why I resigned.'

'To cause interference?'

Hawk gave his superior officer an equally irritated glance. 'Because of that clause in the contract. I thought the only way I could continue a long-term relationship with Charlie was to work in another department. I thought I could go back to detective work.'

'But that's why *I* resigned!' Charlotte exclaimed. 'I was planning to go back to being a paramedic.' Then her jaw dropped as something else Hawk had said finally sank in. 'Long term?' Her tone was one of sheer amazement. 'But a long-term relationship is the *last* thing you want.'

'Who says?'

'*You* did.'

'When?'

'When we had that discussion about falling in love. That night that would have been my anniversary if I'd married Jamie. You said it was just out-of-control hormones and it never lasted.'

'I said you needed time to know whether you had found the right person to spend the rest of your life with.'

'And you said you'd chosen the wrong person and you had no wish to repeat the experience.'

'You were married, Hawk?'

'Engaged,' Hawk told Currie. The distraction was only

momentary. He hadn't taken his eyes off Charlotte. 'Maybe I've found the *right* person this time.'

Charlotte caught her breath. Did that mean...? 'You mean you've changed your mind, Hawk?'

The hint of a smile teased the corners of his mouth. 'No. I knew you were the right person all along. I just didn't recognise it.'

Charlotte shook her head. 'No... I meant, have you changed your mind about falling in love?'

Hawk looked thoughtful. 'I've changed my mind about it being a woman's prerogative to change her mind, too. Doing well, aren't I?'

Lance Currie was resting his forehead against his hands now. Charlotte thought she heard a sigh emanating from behind the desk.

'You resigned from your *job*, Hawk? So that we could continue seeing each other?'

'There's more to life than just work,' Hawk said. He smiled. 'Somebody that I have the greatest respect for told me that so it must be true.' His smile faded. 'Actually, I knew it was true the moment I picked up Sarah's baby that night.'

Charlotte felt the prickle of potential tears but it wasn't just the thought of that baby that touched her so deeply.

'Yeah,' Hawk repeated softly. 'I changed my mind.'

'Why didn't you tell me?'

'And have you taken off because I wanted all the things you didn't want? That the game we were playing had become one I wanted to play for keeps?' Hawk raised his eyebrows. 'Hello?'

Charlotte could feel a smile beginning to shape her lips.

'And there was the little problem of you still being in love with Jamie,' Hawk added. 'I had him staring at me from your desk every day to remind me that I'd never have a chance.' He stopped abruptly and his brow creased. 'Actually, I haven't seen that photograph recently. What have you done with it?'

'Put it away,' Charlotte told him. 'Where it belongs… with other old memories. How I felt about Jamie is ancient history now, Hawk.' Her smile grew a little. 'Someone *I* respect very much told me that if you shut passion away for too long, something inside will wither and die. He also told me it was time I started living again.'

'Well, this is all very well and I'm delighted for you both.' Lance Currie sounded anything but delighted. 'Rules are rules, however, and I can't allow a two-person department to be having a carry-on like this. Unless…'

'Unless?' Hawk and Charlotte both turned surprised faces towards Currie.

'Unless there's some kind of guarantee that it's not going to completely undermine the efficient functioning of the SCS.'

'There are no guarantees in life,' Hawk said slowly. 'You have to make the most of every moment of joy you can get.' He wasn't looking at his superior officer now. His gaze had locked with Charlotte's. 'And if being with one person creates more joy than anything else in your life then you have to do everything you can to hang onto that. To make it last just as long as you can. To make it better even. Stronger.'

'Well, *I* want some kind of guarantee,' Currie said firmly. 'At least an indication of commitment so I won't be waiting for you two to fall out and be trying to work together without speaking to each other. For heaven's sake, would it be too much to ask for you two lovebirds to get married? Or at least *engaged*.'

'Oh…I don't think that would be too much to ask.' Charlotte's gaze was still locked on Hawk's. 'Do you, Hawk?'

The love she could see reflected in his dark eyes chased away any remnants of fear for their future.

'No,' Hawk said mildly. 'I don't think that's too much to ask at all.'

'So you'll get engaged, then?' Currie pressed. 'Now?'

'No.'

Charlotte raised her eyebrows in dismay at Hawk's decisive tone. Currie buried his face in his hands and groaned.

'We'll get married,' Hawk announced. 'If that's OK with my partner, that is.'

Charlotte gulped. 'It's fine with me.'

Currie groaned again. 'Well, that's just peachy. Rush into it, why don't you? Next thing it'll be babies that are disrupting my department.' He raised his head and gave Charlotte's stomach a suspicious glance.

Charlotte and Hawk just smiled at each other.

'I suppose…' Currie said grudgingly. 'We could offer Cam his job back when he wants it. By then, I expect Charlie will either be the size of a house or I will have persuaded the powers that be that the workload of the SCS does, in fact, require a three-person team.' He pushed himself to his feet. 'And I suppose I'd better give you two a few minutes to celebrate your engagement, however brief that turns out to be.' He had the two letters of resignation in his hand. 'I take it I can put these in the shredder?'

Charlotte and Hawk smiled at him.

'Fine.' Currie paused when he reached the door. 'You've got two minutes,' he told them. 'Then I want some evidence that the working of this department will continue without further interruptions.'

The two minutes became three. And then five. It was the longest and most satisfying kiss Charlotte had ever experienced.

'I love you,' Hawk murmured when they finally pulled back far enough to see each other's faces.

'I love you, too, Hawk. *So* much.'

'We don't have to get married, you know. I just said that to keep Elsie happy.'

'*Did* you?'

'No.' Hawk pulled Charlotte into a tight hug. 'I said it because it's what *I* want. More than I've ever wanted anything. I was just trying to give you an escape clause in case it wasn't what you wanted.'

'Oh…' Charlotte raised her face for another kiss. 'Then don't worry, Hawk. Marrying you is exactly what I want.'

The door to the office opened and a sigh was heard. 'I see you two haven't finished *fluffing* around yet.' Currie's gruff tone could not disguise a surprising level of tolerance, possibly even approval, at what was happening in his office. 'I'll give you another two minutes, then.'

Hawk grinned. 'Make it ten.'

Christmas is a time for miracles...

Christmas Deliveries

Caroline Anderson   Marion Lennox

Sarah Morgan

On sale 3rd December 2004

Available at most branches of WHSmith, Tesco, ASDA, Martins, Borders, Eason, Sainsbury's and all good paperback bookshops.

_Medical
romance™

ASSIGNMENT: CHRISTMAS by Caroline Anderson
(Audley Memorial)

A&E consultant Tom Whittaker is Sister Fliss Ryman's perfect man – and with four children to bring up alone, he is the most committed man she knows! He has no intention of taking on more commitment, but their shared needs tempt them into a passionate affair – strictly no strings. And then Fliss becomes pregnant!

THE POLICE DOCTOR'S DISCOVERY
by Laura MacDonald (Police Surgeons)

When Dr Rachel Beresford returns home as locum GP and police doctor, she's surprised that Nick Kowalski still lives there. Her former boyfriend is now a senior police officer, and the powerful connection they once shared quickly surfaces. As an investigation gets underway and a threat is made to Rachel's life, she finds herself seeking safety in Nick's arms...

THE NURSE'S WEDDING RESCUE by Sarah Morgan

(Lakeside Mountain Rescue)

The moment GP Dr Oliver Hunter saw Helen Forrester at his sister's wedding he fell head over heels. But Helen was nursing a broken heart and was against men *and* marriage. Oliver was used to mending all things broken, and soon had Helen working with him on a dangerous mountain rescue. He knew that when life was on the line you made every second count!

On sale 3rd December 2004

Available at most branches of WHSmith, Tesco, ASDA, Martins, Borders, Eason, Sainsbury's and all good paperback bookshops.

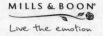

<u>WE VALUE YOUR OPINION!</u>

YOUR CHANCE TO WIN A ONE YEAR SUPPLY OF YOUR FAVOURITE BOOKS.

If you are a regular UK reader of Mills & Boon® Medical Romance™ and have always wanted to share your thoughts on the books you read—here's your chance:

Join the Reader Panel today!

This is your opportunity to let us know exactly what you think of the books you love.

And there's another great reason to join:

Each month, all members of the Reader Panel have a chance of winning four of their favourite Mills & Boon romance books EVERY month for a whole year!

If you would like to be considered for the Reader Panel, please complete and return the following application. Unfortunately, as we have limited spaces, we cannot guarantee that everyone will be selected.

Name: _____

Address: _____

_____ Post Code: _____

Home Telephone: _____ Email Address: _____

Where do you normally get your Mills & Boon Medical Romance books (please tick one of the following)?

Shops   ❑   Library/Borrowed   ❑

Reader Service™   ❑   If so, please give us your subscription no. _____

Please indicate which age group you are in:

16 – 24   ❑   25 – 34   ❑

35 – 49   ❑   50 – 64   ❑   65 +   ❑

If you would like to apply by telephone, please call our friendly Customer Relations line on **020 8288 2886**, or get in touch by email to readerpanel@hmb.co.uk

Don't delay, apply to join the Reader Panel today and help ensure the range and quality of the books you enjoy.

Send your application to:

**The Reader Service, Reader Panel Questionnaire,
FREEPOST NAT1098, Richmond, TW9 1BR**

If you do not wish to receive any additional marketing material from us, please contact the Data Manager at the address above.

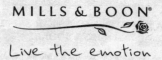

MILLS & BOON®

Live the emotion

A Christmas Engagement

A time for giving…and receiving – a ring

**In December 2004 By Request brings back
three festive favourites by our bestselling
Mills & Boon authors:**

Claiming His Child *by Margaret Way*
A Nanny for Christmas *by Sara Craven*
Lisa's Christmas Assignment
by Jessica Matthews

A perfect Christmas…the perfect gift…

Make sure you pick up your **'perfect
Christmas gift'** which will be on sale from
Friday 3rd December 2004

FREE

4 BOOKS AND A SURPRISE GIFT!

We would like to take this opportunity to thank you for reading this Mills & Boon® book by offering you the chance to take FOUR more specially selected titles from the Medical Romance™ series absolutely FREE! We're also making this offer to introduce you to the benefits of the Reader Service™—

- ★ **FREE home delivery**
- ★ **FREE gifts and competitions**
- ★ **FREE monthly Newsletter**
- ★ **Books available before they're in the shops**
- ★ **Exclusive Reader Service offers**

Accepting these FREE books and gift places you under no obligation to buy; you may cancel at any time, even after receiving your free shipment. Simply complete your details below and return the entire page to the address below. You don't even need a stamp!

YES! Please send me 4 free Medical Romance books and a surprise gift. I understand that unless you hear from me, I will receive 6 superb new titles every month for just £2.69 each, postage and packing free. I am under no obligation to purchase any books and may cancel my subscription at any time. The free books and gift will be mine to keep in any case.

M4ZEE

Ms/Mrs/Miss/Mr..Initials ....

BLOCK CAPITALS PLEASE

Surname ....

Address ....

....

....Postcode ....

Send this whole page to:

The Reader Service, FREEPOST CN81, Croydon, CR9 3WZ